Rosy

SARAH RICHMOND

First Edition: Brides of Serendipity Copyright © 2008 Sarah Richmond
Revised Edition, Rosy, copyright 2018 by Sarah Richmond

Electronic edition: ISBN-13: 978-0-9861671-5-7
Print edition: ISBN-13: 978-1-7332573-2-9

Dedication

This book is dedicated to Avery Allen

Acknowledgements

Just outside Fallon, Nevada on Route 50 on the way to Carson City, stands a Nevada Historical Marker for Ragtown. It is all that remains of the once thriving town. The people who lived there were as diverse as the American landscape. They are now part of American history. My hope is they will be remembered for their hard work, physical and moral courage and family loyalty. Together, they built a nation.

Many thanks to the Fallon, Nevada Tourism Office for their help and interest in this project. Also to the Mark Twain Bookstore in Virginia City, Nevada for their suggestions. For more information about the State of Nevada and the interesting places to see there, please try www.travelnevada.com.

Rosy

Chapter One

S IX RAPID BLASTS shattered the morning's calm. Rosamund Sherry pushed the frying pan to the back of the stove. Jake had taken breakfast down to Will Cannon and the prisoner, a youngster from St. Louis who'd been caught stealing a horse out of Mr. Beaver's livery. The shots came from that direction.

She hurried to the front door. Her hand rested on the doorknob, trembling from the known and unknown. Her husband of five months, the Sheriff of Ragtown, Churchill County, State of Nevada, carried his father's LeMat double barrel nine shot. His deputy, Will, packed a Navy Colt. Six shots meant a gunfight. Somebody was hurt or worse.

Jake had told her time and time again to stay inside when she heard shots ring out. This corner of Nevada was a land that resisted taming, he'd warned her. Lawless men roamed these hills and valleys and they found a settlement of law-abiding citizens easy prey.

So Rosamund left the door closed and locked it. Taking a seat in her parlor, she wrung her hands instead.

From the window she saw Cal Turner's boy, Jason, run

up the street carrying his pa's Winchester. The look of determination on his face matched the growing dread that gripped Rosamund. As agonizing as the sound of gunfire was, the waiting that followed tested the most patient person's resolve. Rosamund Sherry had never been patient.

Jason Turner slipped into the Mercantile, his first concern to check on the safety of his mother and father. Jason, even at the tender age of twelve, wouldn't ignore his duty to defend his town and family.

Rosamund hadn't objected when Jake told her he wanted to leave Virginia behind and take up a new life out West. The War had damaged them all and he wanted a fresh start in a place where he could keep the peace.

The lawlessness that came with the push westward was being tamed by men like her husband, seasoned in battle and decent to their core.

The town, called of all things Ragtown, had grown up around fresh water, a tiny oasis that the wagon trains made for before their ascent over the Sierra Nevada mountains and on into California.

The town had been swept away by the Carson River in the spring of 1862. Settled by folks with determination and grit, the citizens of Ragtown had built again and shaped the land to create a place that withstood nature's fury. Now in the year of our Lord, 1871, in the renewal that was spring, Jake and Rosamund decided this was as good place as any to settle down and raise a family.

Rosamund fidgeted with the hem of her apron. She hadn't thought she'd take to domestic life but cooking over the cast-iron stove and keeping her own home made her happy. She'd added her own feminine touches to the house Jake built but cooking gave her the most pleasure. Seeing her husband's face light up when he sat down to a home-cooked meal gladdened her heart.

Where was Jake? Why hadn't he come home to reassure her everything was all right?

Rosamund couldn't abide the waiting any longer. She put on her bonnet and checked her appearance in the hall mirror. She didn't recognize herself. She was no longer a belle of the South, a girl in hoop skirts and silk finery but a pioneer woman in calico and sensible shoes.

Despite Jake's warning and knowing full well he'd be angry, Rosamund slid the bolt free and opened the door. The street was empty. She stepped outside and closed the door behind her. Her nerves tingled a warning, but she had to know what had happened.

She walked as quickly as decorum would allow to the side street where they'd built the jailhouse. People hid in the doorways of their businesses. The window of the Mercantile was crowded with faces straining to see what had happened. She turned the corner and saw a covey of men mingled outside the jailhouse. When she arrived at Jake's office, she maintained an outward appearance of calm and civility toward the crowd of men, two qualities she'd learned from her mother. A lady never rushed and she remembered her manners at every occasion.

When the men recognized her, they stepped back and gave her ample room to make her way up the steps to the boardwalk. They clutched their hats to their chests, a gesture she found endearing in this rough-and-tumble crowd.

She reached the closed door, aware of the eerie silence. She heard her own ragged breathing and the pounding of her heart as she looked back at the men for an explanation. No one spoke. Some of them bowed their heads.

She lifted the cast-iron latch on the door of the sheriff's

office. The door squeaked on tired hinges.

Dr. McKinnon was putting his instruments into his black leather bag. He didn't look up to greet her. Will Cannon stood next to him.

Jake had been laid out on the big oak desk he'd been given by the retiring sheriff, Henry Barrett, before he and his wife left to visit her family in the old country.

His eyes were half open. She expected him to break out into that lazy smile that made her feel special.

There was no recognition in his eyes. There'd be no gentle admonishment that everything was all right and she shouldn't have come.

The smile and kind spirit had been silenced forever. Jake's shirt was riddled with holes the size of Liberty dimes. His gun wasn't in its holster, which hung over his chair.

She gazed inquiringly at Will but he looked away. Jake's gun should be there. Why wasn't his gun in his holster?

Rosamund was conscious of the odor of gunpowder and blood. She didn't cover her nose with her delicate, lacy handkerchief, which she kept in her pocket when the odors of the rural town became unbearable. She wanted to remember this smell.

"I'm sorry," Will said, at last, putting his hand on her shoulder.

Rosamund shook out of his grasp, his consolation unbearable. Her hands tightened into fists.

"The Kid got a jump on us," Will explained. "I don't know how. It happened real fast. Jake didn't have a chance."

Rosamond's eyes stung from hot tears and her lower lip trembled. She didn't believe him. Jake wouldn't be so careless.

"Take her home," Dr. McKinnon said.

Will's firm hand grasped her waist. She allowed this liberty. Her legs had turned to cornmeal mush and her mind went cloudy as the walls of the room closed in and shock claimed her.

Jason Turner burst into the room, his face and neck dappled red, all twelve years of him ready for a fight.

Rosamund didn't want the boy to see Jake like this. She pulled away from Will to block the view of her husband.

"Will you walk me home?" Rosamund asked with some semblance of self-control.

Jason searched the faces of the men in the room and then nodded. "Yes, ma'am."

Rosamund took his arm. Jason straightened to his full height and tucked the rifle under his other arm. With as much dignity as she could muster, she left the body of the only man she ever loved to the consideration of those he'd vowed to serve and protect.

THE GOOD PEOPLE of Ragtown tried to fill the void that comes after a devastating loss with kind words, loving remembrances and covered casseroles. A void remained in the pit of Rosamund's stomach, a hollowness that would never be filled.

There were days when she couldn't get out of bed. The stove which she'd taken so much pride in cooking on had gone cold.

Jake's death had stripped her of her emotional bearings. Day-to-day living became a chore instead of a joy.

Rosamund Sherry knew instinctively that she'd lost the

love of her life and at the tender age of twenty-two, the best years of her life were behind her.

After that day, everybody called Jake's killer the Kid. Nobody knew his name and few outside of Will Cannon had seen his face.

Except Rosamund had seen his face. Bitten by curiosity, she'd looked through the window of the jailhouse when the Kid had been taken prisoner. She'd seen a boy of eighteen and had actually felt sorry for him.

The air crackled with gossip and speculation about what happened that morning at the jailhouse. How had the Kid gotten hold of Jake's gun? How had he gotten away?

Their questions, no matter how well intentioned, hurt Rosamund. Jake had never been careless a day in his life. He'd been methodical and precise. He'd survived four years in the Virginia Light Infantry.

What the Union Army had failed to do, the Kid had done in one terrible, swift moment. Nobody could explain why, least of all her.

She'd sent word to her family and Jake's mother and father back in Richmond. The message had been brief with the promise that she'd send details later.

The days passed slowly until a week had gone by, and then another one. One bright morning she heard a knock at her door. Jason stood in the doorway holding a letter in his hand. He looked at her with concern, his youthful energy quelled out of respect for her.

"This letter's been waiting for you down at the stage agent's office," Jason said. "I told him it wasn't any trouble for me to deliver it in person."

She thanked him and took the letter that had come all the way from Richmond, Virginia.

"You won't be leaving Ragtown?" Jason asked anxiously, his gaze on the letter in her hand.

"I don't know," she answered truthfully.

"I...we all hope you'll stay."

"Thank you," she said.

She watched him walk away, kicking a stone in front of him. He'd been such a Godsend since that awful morning and afterward helping her split wood for the kitchen stove and hauling water from the well.

They'd all been helpful. They all wanted her to stay.

Rosamund shut the door and took a seat in the parlor. She recognized her mother's handwriting. She broke the seal and opened the expensive vellum. When she took out the pages, the familiar scents of home aroused tender affections for the sender. As she'd thought, her mother begged her to return to her family, fearing for her safety.

She knew they'd insist she return to Virginia. A part of her had already decided that she would. She wanted to sit in the comfort of her parent's veranda again and watch the sun drop behind the gentle, green Virginian countryside.

Ragtown was vulgar and uncivilized. There weren't the amenities of a proper home. Drifters blew in like the hot winds off the desert. Lawlessness had plagued the community ever since the Comstock had played out and many a punter had gone broke.

Could a lady live here, especially alone?

In the company of the people of Ragtown she'd found friends. She had the house Jake had built. Something deep inside her told her she would be disloyal to Jake's memory if she left, that their dream of a new life would never be fulfilled if she cut and ran.

Rosamund put her mother's letter down on the hall table and went into the kitchen. Morning sun filled the room. She stood there a moment basking in its warmth.

She'd lived in a fog long enough and she needed to make some decisions.

She found a piece of paper and sat own at the pretty mahogany desk that had been freighted all the way from Fort Worth. As she dipped her pen in ink, she tried to find the words to put her family's concerns at ease. Words couldn't convey her attachment to the small town but she did her best.

Regretfully, her parents would never agree that their daughter should stay so far away by herself. So she promised to reconsider her decision if she found living here too difficult.

She sealed the envelope with the last of the wax she'd brought with her from Richmond and rose from her seat. It was already Thursday. The stagecoach would be arriving any minute and she must hurry if she wanted to post her letter.

She tied the long ribbons of her black hat under her chin, drew on kid gloves, and hurried out the door.

Rosamund spotted Mr. Turner sweeping the boardwalk in front of the Mercantile. He stopped when he saw her and waved. She waved back. He leaned on his broom as she approached.

"Good morning," she said, picking up her skirt so the material wouldn't snag on the rough-sawn wood of the boardwalk.

Mr. Turner set the broom against the irregular cut siding of the Mercantile and suspended his thumbs in his braces.

"Nice to see you out," he replied. When he saw the letter in her hand, he eyed it with arched brows.

"I've come to send a letter to my mother and father by the next stage," she said, responding to his gaze.

"It'll be along any time now. The new sheriff's riding with old Angus McFarland and that foolhardy boy who rides shotgun. Come on inside out of the sun, Mrs. Jake."

"A new sheriff?" she asked. She'd missed this bit of news. They'd gone and hired a new sheriff and she hadn't been told.

"A new man is coming from Fort Kearny," Mr. Turner said as if reading her thoughts.

Rosamund wasn't surprised. Will Cannon certainly was a competent deputy but he had his hands full with the lawlessness that plagued their community.

Mr. Turner held the door open for her and she went into the Mercantile.

The room smelled of sawdust. Her gaze fell on the colorful bolts of cotton. There was no having such a fine piece of cloth for a dress. She needed to economize.

"Can I get you a cool drink of water?" Mr. Turner asked.

Rosamund shook her head. "No, thank you." She turned away to look out the window. The smallest kindness put her perilously close to tears. She didn't want to fall apart in front of Mr. Turner. She didn't want to put the poor man in a state of distress because of her.

"I can take that letter over to the stage for you," Mr. Turner said. "No use waiting."

"Thank you for the offer but I'll take it myself." Managing to pull herself together, she faced him squarely.

Mr. Turner kept glancing at the letter.

"You've been so kind, all of you and I thank you for all your many considerations for my welfare. I'm feeling better and I've written a letter telling my family that I intend to stay in Ragtown for now."

Before Mr. Turner could reply, Alice Turner came out

of the back room, tying on a clean apron.

"Good morning, Rosamund," she said. "I didn't know you were here."

Mrs. Turner gave her a quick maternal assessment.

"Hello, Alice," she replied.

"It's so good to see you out of your house."

Rosamund smiled. The smile felt foreign to her. "Thank you. Where's Jason?"

"Where he's run off to, I'll be bound if I know. No doubt practicing with that new rifle of his." She shot her husband a tolerant look.

"He'll be 'round shortly," Mr. Turner replied. "Anything you need that boy for, don't you hesitate to ask."

"Thank you. He's been so helpful."

"Is there anything I can do for you?" Mrs. Turner asked.

"No, actually I'm here to meet the stage."

Mrs. Turner exchanged glances with her husband.

"Mrs. Jake is mailing a letter to her family," Mr. Turner explained.

"I've come to a decision," she explained. "I've told my mother and father that I'm staying in Ragtown for the time being." She didn't know why she added the qualifier. Did she doubt her own abilities to live in this western land? Was she admitting she lacked the backbone to face the same hardships these people faced?

"For the time being" was too convenient an escape. Her lack of commitment troubled her.

As if she guessed, Alice Turner came around the counter and gave Rosamund a quick hug.

"How happy I am, we both are."

Alice Turner's affections brought Rosamund to the brink of fresh tears. Rosamund thought she would be stronger, that the conversations that inevitably turned around her would be easier.

"These things take time." Alice patted her shoulder. "I'm glad you're trying."

Rosamund dabbed at her eyes with the handkerchief she'd retrieved from her sleeve. "Forgive me. I hadn't realized how difficult a simple walk into town to mail a letter would be."

Alice rested her hand on Rosamund's shoulder. "You may not think so but each day will be better than the last."

Rosamund took comfort from her words but doubted she'd ever shed the leaden weight of grief she carried around with her.

"Thank you. Thank you for everything."

"You're as thin as a rail," Alice said with disapproval. "You're not eating proper."

Food had lost importance to Rosamund and she never seemed to have an appetite.

"We'll soon put you right. I'll have Jason bring you some fresh eggs for your supper as soon as I corral that boy."

"Thank you but that's not necessary." Rosamund again teetered on the edge of an emotional drop-off.

"It's no trouble," Alice replied, mistaking Rosamund's refusal as inconvenience. "You'll have your strength back in no time."

Rosamund smiled weakly. She'd not even the strength to argue.

"Now that's settled," Alice said. She looked at her husband. Mr. Turner nodded. "There's something we've been meaning to ask you, me and Mr. Turner."

Rosamund searched their faces. The Turners looked in agreement about something of importance.

Alice elbowed her husband.

Mr. Turner drew himself up as if to give a speech he'd obviously rehearsed. "With the town growing and all and new folks coming from back East, well we thought it was time the town had a school. You know how much Jason thinks of you. We were wondering if you'd take up teaching our young people?"

"Me?" They'd caught her off guard. She hadn't ever considered taking a job.

"You being educated," Mr. Turner added quickly.

Alice turned a gentle smile on Rosamund. "I can't think of a better schoolmarm."

"Where would we have classes?" Rosamond asked.

"At the church," Alice said. "Leastways until a school can be built. Mr. Turner and I have decided to donate an acre of land for the new schoolhouse."

Rosamund had to admit that she liked the idea of Ragtown's very own school.

"You know how Jason loves to read," Alice continued before Rosamund could answer yes or no. "He's mastered his numbers since he's to take over the Mercantile when he's old enough but there's other things that are important to learn. Don't you agree?"

Rosamund lifted her gaze to the woman's earnest face. "Yes, I do agree but I don't know what to say. I don't know if I'm ready to take on a job."

Alice, true to her supportive self, didn't press. "You take all the time you need to decide. School won't be starting until September."

"I will," Rosamund promised. September seemed a long ways away.

Alice gave her a quick hug. She was generous with her hugs and kindness itself. She'd thought of Rosamund when considering their very first schoolteacher. Rosamund appreciated the woman's confidence in her abilities.

Rosamund heard the thunder of hooves.

Mr. Turner took out his pocket watch and looked at the time. "That'll be the stage."

"The new sheriff is due this morning," Alice said haltingly. She too, was solicitous of Rosamund's feelings on the matter of a new sheriff.

"Yes, Mr. Turner told me. I'm so very glad the town fathers have found a satisfactory sheriff in a timely fashion."

"He's a Yankee," Alice said with a frown. "I can't abide by them that fought for the Union. If you ask me, they can't be trusted."

So that was why no one had told her about the new sheriff, Rosamond thought. They were correct in assuming her loyalties were well-rooted in Southern soil and didn't want to cause her any additional distress.

"Now Alice, don't be saying such things." Mr. Turner's tone was stern. "The war is over and it's time to put such talk behind us."

Alice's mouth pinched severely, ready with a stiff rebuke. In deference to Rosamund and much to Mr. Turner's obvious relief, she held her tongue.

There'd be no welcome from her, Rosamund decided. As for her own disposition about having a Yankee sheriff, she couldn't be as quick as Mr. Turner to bury the past.

Mr. Turner opened the door and let the ladies go first. As she passed, he bowed, an old-fashioned gesture of civility. Rosamund's heavy heart was lighter for a moment.

She saw the cloud of dust thrown up by the stage. The weather was unusually dry for this time of year. As the stagecoach driver pulled the team to a walk, Rosamond felt a jump in her pulse. The arrival of the stagecoach always brought news, good and bad. It was a lifeline to the places beyond Ragtown, to the homes they'd left behind and the families they would most likely never see again.

Another man sat next to the stagecoach driver. He carried a rifle across his lap. Rosamund knew full well that meant the stage carried a strong box. Both men's faces were covered with red bandanas, a defense against the dust.

Another man sat with his back to them, his hat pulled down low. Rosamund guessed this was the new sheriff.

A sheriff was essential to the town. She firmly believed in the rule of law and knew Ragtown would thrive and grow only if law-abiding citizens were protected. She realized she must be civil even if he was a Yankee.

The stage came to a halt in front of the Wells Fargo agent's office. She crossed the street with the Turners behind her. She wanted to be the first to welcome the new sheriff. As the widow of Jake Sherry, she wanted the sheriff to know civilized people lived in this corner of Nevada and the citizens of Ragtown knew their manners.

The horses shuddered and stamped their hooves. Rosamund stepped up on to the boardwalk. A saddled bay with four white stockings, tied to the back of the stage, pulled back on his reins, his eyes wide with excitement.

"Whoa," came a man's strong baritone voice and Rosamund looked up. A tall man jumped down to the ground. He untied the reins and led the nervous animal to a hitching post. With a gentling hand, he patted the horse's neck.

"Good morning," Rosamund said, stepping forward.

The man turned and looked at her with startlingly golden eyes flecked with defiance. He looked frighteningly like an outlaw with his face partially covered with a red bandana and wearing a dusty black hat.

He wore chaps around his wool trousers and a dark blue shirt with two rows of brass buttons. His gun belt sat low on his hip with a six-shooter at the ready.

He pulled the mask down and gave her an assessing gaze that made her uncomfortable.

The top half of his face was caked with grime and the bottom half needed a shave. He'd the burnished coloring of a man who lived outdoors. No doubt he slept on the hard ground and ate out of the pan he fried his dinner in.

In contrast, his mouth was soft and sensuous. Among the rugged planes of his face shone the reckless charm of a man who didn't take no for an answer.

Rosamund considered herself an excellent judge of character and she decided the new sheriff would look out of place in a lady's parlor but he'd never be out of place in a lady's bed.

"I'm Rosamund Sherry," she said and she stuck out her gloved hand.

He shook her hand with a firm grasp. "Matthew Kincaid. You must be Jake Sherry's wife."

"Yes and now I'm his widow."

"I was sorry to hear about what'd happened."

Rosamund appreciated him saying so. "Did you know my husband?"

"No, ma'am but I heard he was a mighty fine sheriff and a good man."

"Thank you, Mr. Kincaid, he was indeed a very good man."

Matthew Kincaid turned his attention to his horse and loosened the cinch on the saddle.

"I guess I'm the welcoming committee of one,"

Rosamund said, looking around. The others were busy unloading the stagecoach and waiting on the stage agent for their mail and packages.

He pulled off the saddle and rested it on his hip. He led the horse in the direction of the water trough.

Rosamund walked with him. She wanted him to know how important his taking this job was to the people of Ragtown.

"Mr. Kincaid," she said, "you need to know this is a good town with good people. We're all trying to establish a civilized corner in the State of Nevada."

Sheriff Kincaid shrugged. "My primary reason for being here is to find your husband's killer."

"I would be most grateful. We all hope for justice."

"Seems to me, justice plays no part in it. I was hired to do some killing."

Rosamund was taken back by the coldness of his reply. "Naturally, if it comes to that but you should know we don't allow gunfights in our town and we won't condone any unnecessary violence."

Matthew Kincaid stopped at the water trough and let his horse drink. "Ma'am, gun fighting is what I do best."

Rosamund shuddered. The new sheriff thought he had the job figured out. She and Jake had come to Ragtown to change the lawless frontier into a place where decent law-abiding citizens could live peacefully and raise a family. The days of gun fighting were in the past.

"There are better ways to deal with outlaws," she replied. "Respectable people demand it."

He pushed his horse away from the water. "There's only one way to deal with men like the Kid. One of us is going to die."

It was a terrible price to pay for a tin star, Rosamund

knew, and one she couldn't accept.

She looked at him more closely. She didn't see a man prepared to die so the only other explanation was that he was supremely confident. Sheriff Kincaid must not have a conscience, especially when it came to taking another man's life.

"Please don't think you must kill the Kid on my account."

He cupped his hand in the horse trough and washed his face and neck. The water dripped off the curly hairs of his mustache. He wiped his face with the bandana. When he finished, he looked down at her. "I'm thinking it's on Sheriff Sherry's account that I'm here."

Rosamund stiffened her spine. He was plain-spoken and he'd put her in her place. "Yes, of course."

"You fixin' to go back home?" He looked at the letter in her hand.

"In fact, I'm not. I plan to stay here in Ragtown." She didn't add "for a while".

"You shouldn't be here."

"What is that supposed to mean?"

"Pampered females don't belong in a town like this."

"I'm not pampered," she said, indignant at his assumption.

"You ever shoot a gun?"

"There hadn't been any need."

"How 'bout cut the neck off a rooster?"

"Well, no."

"Poke a pig? Chop wood? Lance a blister?"

"What is your point?"

"Seems to me I've made my point." She saw a twitch that could be interpreted as a smile or as close to a smile men such as Sheriff Kincaid could manage. She saw in that smile some inner conviction about females.

She raised her head. She bruised easily these days but Mr. Kincaid's unkind words didn't bring on a fit of tears. To cry at his insults would only strengthen his case.

"Good day, sir," she said.

She turned and started walking, hating the conversation, hating how the man made her blood percolate. She walked all the way home feeling his gaze follow her.

The stagecoach pulled away and she still held the letter in her hand. She turned around, exasperated that she could've been so distracted.

The sheriff and his horse had disappeared.

Rosamund had good reason to scold herself. She'd gotten riled by the man's simple take on what must be a very dangerous way of living. Matthew Kincaid had come to their town to find Jake's killer. He'd told her there was more killing ahead, plain and simple.

Much as she hoped he was wrong, she couldn't hold his opinions against him.

The inside of her house was cooler. She dropped the envelope on the hall table and untied her bonnet. She'd mail the letter when the stage came through next week.

Sheriff Kincaid was no gentleman, she decided. He was uncouth and formed a first impression before she'd even had a chance to prove herself. He thought her too fragile a Southern flower, a judgment she intended to prove wrong.

She wouldn't let him bully her.

She belonged in Ragtown as much as anybody else.

Chapter Two

ROSAMUND STIRRED A kettle of venison stew on top of the cast-iron stove. They'd gotten off to a bad start, the new sheriff and herself but in her experience, all fences could be mended with a good meal.

The odor of red meat cooking upset her stomach and the heat from the stove added to her discomfort. She sat down in a kitchen chair and fanned herself with a kitchen towel.

Matthew Kincaid was an experienced gunfighter, and she'd realized after some reflection, a professional would be single-minded when it came to hunting down cold-blooded killers. Any man worthy of the badge would be of the same opinion.

She'd spoken out of turn, telling him how to do his job.

The stew bubbled and spat. Rosamund rose from the chair and covered the steaming pot with a heavy lid.

The man had been living rough. A woman's way of doing things could be counted on to soothe a jagged soul. She packed a white damask serviette, one from a set she'd brought with her from Richmond, into a wicker basket. She tucked one of her very best china plates, cup and saucer and a gleaming sterling silver fork and spoon wrapped in another snowy white serviette on top. Matthew Kincaid would see these touches of civilization and come to appreciate them, she felt sure.

As she tied on her bonnet, she decided it felt good to be busy.

She'd thought long and hard about the Millers' offer. Becoming the town's school teacher suited her. Caring for and educating the children of this town would be her calling.

She lugged the kettle outside and placed it in her wagon. She added a freshly brewed pot of coffee and her basket. Lastly, she carried out a pitcher of hot water, a bar of store-bought soap and a thick, white towel.

Her effort gave her a sense of satisfaction. She couldn't wait to see the look on Sheriff Kincaid's face.

The town bustled with activity. Rosamund didn't try to suppress a heartfelt smile even though she was draped in black.

She waved at the many people she counted as friends. They waved back. She realized how much she'd missed greeting these fine people with pleasantries and sharing the news of the day. Many of them had traveled by wagon train across the emigrant trail. Many had walked from faraway places. Rosamund's journey had been difficult, coming across by the transcontinental railroad but it hadn't been as harrowing as what others had faced.

Every one of them watched her with curiosity as she pulled the heavy wagon.

When she reached the sheriff's office, she left the wagon in the street and climbed the boardwalk. She hadn't been near the sheriff's office since Jake died. The events of that morning were burned into her consciousness with harsh clarity and deep sorrow.

She touched the door latch and swallowed grief and despair as the memory came flooding back. Maybe this was too soon. With as much willpower as she could muster, she push through the revulsion and dread and opened the door.

Rosamund blinked as her eyes adjusted to the dim light. The small window that faced the street was cast in shadows at this time of the day.

She saw the sheriff asleep on the cot in the single jail cell. He was long and lanky and his black hat covered his face. His legs were crossed at the ankles. Surprisingly, he wore his boots as he slept.

She looked at the big oak desk where Jake had died, at the bullet holes in the adobe bricks behind it. She'd expected to see bloodstains but the desk and adobe had been scrubbed clean.

She didn't let her feelings paralyze her as they'd done in the past couple of months.

She had to move forward, to find her own way now that Jake was gone.

Rosamund brought in the food. She worked quickly and quietly. When all was ready, when the desk was set with a king's fare, she went over to the cell.

Matthew Kincaid's chest rose and fell with each throaty rumble. His holster was draped over the iron bedpost within easy reach. The man was dead tired and looked as helpless as a kitten. What wore him out she could only guess. Rosamund hated to wake the man who looked so peaceful. She stepped back and pondered what to do.

The room already held the aroma of venison and thick gravy, buttermilk biscuits and freshly churned butter. Even the pungency of coffee made of black chicory added to the delicious smells.

She backed up to the door and stood with the back of her head pressed against the rough-sawn wood. She lifted the latch, having made the decision to leave and return later.

The metallic click of the latch brought Sheriff Kincaid to his feet. His hat tumbled to the floor. With lightning speed, he'd drawn his gun from its holster and aimed it at the middle of her chest.

His face was as cold as the steel in his hand.

A cry rose in her throat and she raised her hand to shield her face.

A look of recognition softened his features. He dropped his stance and swept a hand over his hair, taming the mane of restless dark curls.

"Don't ever do that again," he said, his voice roaring, commanding.

"I'm sorry," she said, stammering. "You don't have to speak in such a tone."

He shook his head and shucked his gun in its holster. "What are you doing here?"

She pointed at the meal spread out on his desk. "I thought you might like something to eat."

His eyes widened when he saw what she'd done.

"You'll want to wash," she said boldly and turned to fetch the pitcher of hot water in the wagon. Her nerves were shattered. She'd never had a gun held on her before and she understood the sheer terror of being in the line of fire. She could've easily been killed.

Make no mistake. She was in dangerous company.

When she returned, he'd wiped the last vestiges of sleep from his eyes and rolled up his sleeves. Many days' worth of beard made him look dangerous. She poured the water in the white basin and took the piece of green soap out of her pocket. He lathered up the soap and washed his hands and arms. The black hairs on his arms stood up as he rinsed.

She felt a physical attraction that was unwanted and improper.

When he finished, he wiped his hands on the clean cotton towel she'd brought. He tossed the towel aside and rubbed his face with reddened hands. His grizzly disposition had changed.

She smiled with satisfaction at the transformation.

"What's all this?" he asked, his gaze on the kettle of stew.

"Your dinner. My friends and neighbors here in Ragtown say I'm a fair cook," she said.

He lifted the lid and peered inside. "Smells mighty good, but I have to ask myself, what are you after?"

Rosamund was unprepared for such rudeness. His gaze pierced right though her armor of civility.

"I wanted to thank you for taking this job," she replied. "The people of Ragtown deserve protection. I didn't thank you properly this morning."

He set the lid on the desk and straddled the desk chair without uttering one word about his behavior this morning. No apology for how his words had contributed to a widow's distress. Obviously, she'd been expecting too much. "I'll leave you to your dinner. Jason can bring…"

He looked up. "Sit down. We've got business to discuss after I'm done eating."

Rosamund had never been spoken to in such a manner. The sheriff had no consideration for a lady. Nor, apparently, did he appreciate her effort to welcome him.

She carried the chair from the cell and placed it across from Sheriff Kincaid. She sat.

Matthew Kincaid pushed the serviette to one side. He ate with both hands, elbows planted firmly on the table.

He pushed the biscuit around in the meat drippings and popped it into his mouth whole. He smiled at her as he chewed. She wasn't offended. He showed his appreciation the way he knew how.

A part of him, she decided, wanted to goad her into losing her temper. She didn't take the bait. She sat with her hands folded in her lap with a serene, lady-like countenance.

When he finished, he wiped his mouth off using the serviette and belched heartily without excusing himself. He dropped the serviette next to the plate. Tipping back in his chair, he eyed her with casual indifference.

"That was a fine meal, Rosy. My belly agrees with what the folks here in Ragtown are saying about your cooking."

Rosamund smiled, satisfied she'd done the right thing bringing their sheriff a good meal. She hated that he'd abbreviated her name but she didn't say anything for the moment. The name didn't suit her but he'd find that out soon enough.

"Thank you. You're kind to say so."

Her comment brought a crooked smile to his face, adding to his peculiar kind of charm. Rosamund felt a tug at her heart. She shouldn't mistake that gleam in his eye for attraction, for that would be a terrible mistake.

"If I didn't know better, I'd think you were trying to hornswoggle me."

"I assure you I had no such intention."

He looked doubtful. "It ain't fitting that a citizen bribe a town official, especially his first day on the job."

Their gazes met as adversaries. He wanted her to know he was wise to feminine wiles. She didn't look away.

"You and I have a common purpose," she said, "the

welfare of the people of Ragtown. Now that you are a member of our community, I'd be honored to bring you dinner."

He nodded and sat his chair back on the ground. She was glad her words had been accepted for their honesty.

"I do have a question to ask," she said.

He frowned. "What kind of question?"

"You told me you were here to find my husband's killer. Surely the man who shot Jake wouldn't be around this part of Nevada anymore?"

He rested his large hands on the desk. "I don't rightly know where the killer is, Rosy, but I've given the situation some thought."

"Have you come to a conclusion?"

"I have. He's killed a man and I've no doubt he'll kill again."

The possibility of another death sent shivers down her spine.

"The Kid is fast on the draw and foolish enough to prove himself in every cow town he comes across. Once his reputation becomes known, he'll have to prove himself on a regular basis."

"Prove himself to you," she said.

"I'm afraid so. I have a reputation for being quick on the draw."

Rosamund thought it precious little to be proud of.

She stood. "I sincerely hope it won't come to that. If you'll forgive me, I must be leaving."

"Not so fast, Rosy. I've got some questions of my own."

She took a deep breath. It wasn't a question but a demand.

"There's some things about your husband's murder

that don't add up," he said.

Rosamund sank into the chair. She hadn't come here to talk about Jake and that morning. Her hurt was too raw.

The sheriff didn't mince words or try to soften their blow. He had a job to do.

"Did you see Jake's gun that morning?" he asked.

She remembered vividly. "No, his revolver wasn't in his holster."

"It's safe to say the Kid has it."

"I don't know, but clearly Jake never had a weapon to defend himself. He never had a chance."

"How about the deputy?"

Rosamund couldn't remember seeing Will with a gun. Had the Kid gotten the jump on both men? "You'll have to ask him."

Matthew Kincaid nodded. "What bothers me is how the Kid was able to swipe your husband's weapon in the first place."

Everyone in town had wondered the same thing. Rosamund knew this was a missing piece of the puzzle with Jake's reputation on the line.

"There's something you should know about my husband. He wasn't a careless man."

Sheriff Kincaid stroked the coarse whiskers on his chin with his knuckles. "Then the only explanation is the Kid had help."

She appreciated he believed her. He hadn't drawn unfair conclusions as others had.

"But who?" she asked, adding a smile.

He stopped stroking his beard. She'd touched a part of him that he'd been trying to hide. His brief show of interest aroused her curiosity about a man who could be charming one minute and cold as river rock the next.

The moment passed too soon.

"Had to have been someone local," he said sharply.

"That can't be. I know everybody in town. They're all fine people and wouldn't harm Jake."

His look turned cynical. He'd seen the worst in people, she knew, because of the savagery of war.

"I can't talk about this anymore," she said as she stood up.

"Did you see the prisoner?" he asked gruffly.

She couldn't lie even though she'd have to admit to an indiscretion no lady would have undertaken. "I saw him. Jake didn't like me to come down here but I did after the Kid was arrested."

She hadn't told anyone else. Jake treated her like a child at times and she'd wanted to see what a criminal looked like.

"You snuck a peek?" Sheriff Kincaid looked amused.

"I looked in the window," she said.

"Did you get a good look at him?"

"Yes," she confessed.

"I'll need you to give me a description of him."

She didn't want to think about the Kid but the sheriff needed answers.

"He was ordinary looking. Young, maybe eighteen or so. About your height. He wore a red checkered handkerchief around his neck."

Describing Jake's killer gave her goose bumps. The fear and loathing of that morning returned with a vengeance. She began clearing the dishes off his desk.

"Do you think the Kid knows I saw him?" She hurried to pack the basket.

"There's a good possibility and I'm not taking any chances."

She'd defied her husband's specific instructions to stay away from the jail. Now she'd be called on to identify the man who'd taken so much from her.

She picked up the basket and looked into Matthew's eyes. She wasn't afraid.

"We're surely glad you're here," she said sincerely.

He stood up and cupped her hand in his. She couldn't pull away. There was no subtlety to him, no nuance. He knew what he wanted and didn't hesitate to take it.

What shocked her was her response. She felt the blistering heat, the weakness that comes with desire.

"Let me go," she said near panic.

Matthew Kincaid released her and straightened. The atmosphere was charged with emotion.

He made no apology.

"If there's nothing else," she said with a modicum of self-control. "I must be going.

THE INCIDENT AT the jailhouse, as Rosamund chose to call it, had upset her.

There was no denying Matthew Kincaid was irresistible. She'd recognized his physical attributes the moment he'd arrived on the stage. She'd no doubt he took advantage of the many females drawn to him by his reckless charm.

When he'd taken possession of her hand, her skin had heated to dizzying heights.

She was the widow of his predecessor, for heaven's sake. A thread of decency must be preserved.

Men such as Matthew Kincaid didn't understand the inappropriateness of grabbing a lady's hand without her permission. Rosamund would be sure, at some later date, to advise him in this regard.

Folks around town had begun to talk about her daily deliveries of a hot meal to the new sheriff. Even the minister's wife had remarked about how it was time Mrs. Jake got on with her life and shed her black gowns for ones more suitable for her age. Rosamund had to admit she looked forward to pulling the wagon filled with good things to eat down the dusty street even though she enjoyed Matthew's company more than was respectable.

One week to the day later, Rosamund stood in line to post her letter to her family. They'd be unhappy about her decision about staying in Ragtown. She meant to reassure them in frequent letters that she was managing just fine.

The stage arrived on schedule. She waited eagerly with her friends and neighbors for their mail. A crate of schoolbooks had arrived, ordered by Mr. Turner in such haste Rosamund wouldn't dare refuse the post of teacher now.

To her surprise and delight the stage agent had a letter for her. She recognized her mother's delicate writing and clutched the letter from home to her bosom. Those around her nodded their heads.

After securing a promise from Jason Turner to deliver the crate to the church, she hurried home.

She filled the kettle for tea and set it on the stove. Her mother's letters were long and packed with details and Rosamund liked to take her time digesting every bit of information.

Her thoughts drifted, as they often did, to Matthew Kincaid. She'd learned he'd worked as a scout out of Fort Kearny after the War. About the war, he didn't speak at all. Jake and the other men she'd known who'd served in the military didn't talk much about the fighting either. She believed they meant to shield their loved ones from the horrors they'd seen and in some cases done.

Matthew didn't seem to have any family. He didn't speak of a wife or sweetheart. She wondered how such a handsome man had escaped the clutches of no doubt many an amorous female.

He came across as a solitary man. Everyone has a past and most had fond memories. Matthew didn't seem to have either, or at least nothing he was willing to talk about.

They'd been sworn enemies but that seemed like a long time ago. Although people would never forget, they must forgive, Mr. Turner had said. His words were wise, she decided. She was tired of the hating and taking sides.

The water came to a boil and turned to steam, and she poured some through the tea infuser into a ceramic pot. She'd plenty of reasons to hate the Kid, she wouldn't deny it, but if he returned to Ragtown, she prayed his return wouldn't be deadly. She wanted to killing to be over.

Rumors abounded about the Kid. One story told that he'd taken up with a gang of train robbers up north but nobody knew for sure. Another rumor claimed he'd gone to San Francisco. His identity remained a secret. His red-checkered handkerchief became his calling card as he spread fear among law-abiding folks.

What Rosamund did know was that she could identify him, she and Will Cannon. Matthew had been quick to remind her of that fact. Would the Kid return to Ragtown to challenge their sheriff's ability with a gun? Would he be that foolish?

She used a letter opener to tear the seal off the vellum. It came off intact. She would save the wax to be melted down and reused for her answering letter.

The scent of lavender and rose hips invaded her senses and a longing for the comforts of home rose up in her chest. How she ached to hear her mother's sweet voice.

There were five pages of news and she settled down in her chair, a cup of tea at her elbow. She delighted in the antics of her older sister Beth's two children. They were growing up and Rosamund would miss their endearing childhood years. Her younger brother Swift had been admitted to a college over in Alexandria. Rosamund felt the maternal pride as her mother described Swift's change from a boy into a man.

What came next made Rosamund sit up in her chair. Aunt Hester, her father-in-law's sister, meant to come out to Ragtown to accompany Rosamund back to her roots. She couldn't be expected to travel unescorted. Her family feared more and more for her safety as news filtered east about the gangs of outlaws who terrorized the settlers.

Rosamund knew there was more to their concern. They feared for her virtue as a lady living alone in a frontier town.

She wished she could convince them that most of the men in Ragtown were every inch gentleman and treated the ladies with respect. Those who didn't had to account for their behavior to Matthew Kincaid.

She wondered what her father and mother would think of Matthew. Would they consider him untrustworthy because he'd fought for the North? She hoped her father would reserve judgment about a man who so willingly faced his own death to defend the community.

Rosamund chewed her lower lip. From the date on the letter, Aunt Hester was on her way. She put the letter down and took a calming drink of tea. Jake's Aunt Hester

SARAH RICHMOND

would be a force to reckon with.

The dear woman had never married and the general consensus around Richmond was that no man was good enough for Hester. So she involved herself in the lives of her nieces and nephews, a mixed blessing, to be sure. Hester would be sure to criticize the change in Rosamond, not only for the scars and calluses from working over a hot stove and keeping her own house, but also for the once porcelain skin now freckled by the sun. Rosamund lived differently from all her family knew. No doubt Hester would consider this new life unworthy of a lady.

Probably the most difficult thing for Hester to accept would be that Rosamund managed very well by herself.

Rosamund suppressed a sigh. She'd be grateful for the company but Hester was set in her ways and Ragtown was a long way from the tea parties of Richmond.

Even more worrisome—for Rosamund was a worrier like her mother—if what she suspected was true about her condition, Aunt Hester would insist Rosamund go back to Virginia with her. There would be no equivocation about taking the teaching post. Auntie would bully until she'd no recourse but to give in to her demands.

Of course, Hester would never understand Rosamund's fascination with Matthew Kincaid. He was a Yankee and Auntie would never consider him worthy of a Southern lady's hospitality. It would be another secret. The weight of the deception would be a heavy one and Rosamund would have to tread carefully until Hester was gone.

Rosamund took out a pen and paper. She needed to reassure her family once again that she would be all right. Satisfied she'd stated her case in a way they'd understand, she signed her name to the letter with a flourish. By the time it arrived in Richmond, she would be starting her first day at school.

FEELING HAPPIER THAN she'd been in months, Rosamund tied on her bonnet and headed for town. The stage would be arriving any minute. Adolph Bascomb, the retired ranch hand who worked for Mr. Beaver at the livery, waited with a fresh team of horses. Horse-trading was almost as important as water in Nevada. Adolph Bascomb knew more about horses than just about any man she'd ever met.

She'd heard Adolph's mother had been an Indian squaw. He didn't talk about his background. People out west kept their past to themselves. It was surely different from Richmond where a person's lineage could be traced back generations and family crests were proudly displayed in the best homes.

She greeted him with a sincere good morning.

The man touched the brim of his battered hat. "Morning, Mrs. Jake. You're looking very pretty this day."

"Why thank you," Rosamund replied, although she'd never considered wearing black attractive.

Adolph smiled shyly, showing dimples above his scraggily beard.

The team snorted and pawed the arid ground, impatient, she guessed, to be on their way to greener pastures. She thought, with a grimace, that conventional society would dictate she should do the same.

Richmond would be in full summer. The lawn stretching out in front of her father's house beckoned her, all green and lush. She always savored the feel of grass between her toes and the sound of bees in her mother's kitchen garden.

"You waiting on the stage?" Adolph asked.

"Yes, I'm sending a letter to my family," she said, "and my aunt is due to arrive from Richmond, Virginia."

"I'm glad to hear it. A woman like you shouldn't be living alone."

That seemed to be the consensus around Ragtown, she mused. She wished there was a way to convince people otherwise.

"Heard you was starting up a school," he said.

"Yes, I am."

Adolph pushed back his hat and scratched his head. "Don't that beat all. A school right here in Ragtown."

"We'll use the church but one day we'll have a proper schoolhouse," she said with pride.

"That's a sure sign of progress to my way of thinking."

"I couldn't agree more," she said.

"If there's anything you need for that school, anything a'tall, you just give this old boy a holler."

Rosamund smiled. Adolph Bascomb was uneducated but he valued having a school. The young people of Ragtown would learn to read and write and do their numbers. With men like Adolph Bascomb's support and forward thinking, the town would surely prosper.

Chapter Three

M ATTHEW KINCAID CAME out of the sheriff's office
across the street. He'd freshly shaved, trimmed his
mustache and put on a clean shirt. The seven-pointed star
was pinned to a wool vest that was too big for him.

When he saw her, his expression was muted, as if he
couldn't decide if he was glad to see her or not. There
always seemed to be friction between them, something she
couldn't explain and her Southern ways rejected.

He walked toward her, a little bowlegged, his spurs
jingling like a horse in harness.

"Morning, Sheriff," Rosamund said, trying not to
sound coquettish but the sight of the sheriff put her in a
flirtatious frame of mind.

The corners of his mouth turned up slightly. "Morning,
Rosy. You here to meet the stage?"

"I am. My aunt's coming for a visit."

Matthew nodded and walked beside her. His gaze was
on the horizon fringed with distant mountains.

"It's a fine day to be traveling," she said. She'd given
up on flattery to soothe his male sensibilities. The gentle
cajoling of a woman could put a man in a better mood, her
mother often told her. That was before the War, before the
harsh reality of killing and terrible loss, before their world
had turned upside down.

Matthew Kincaid would have none of it. He only tolerated plain talking and so she wouldn't waste her time or his.

"That it is," he replied but he was distracted by those westerly mountains.

"Have you been to California?" she asked.

"Not yet but I mean to go there one day. I hear there's plenty to see out that way."

She'd wondered if he'd stay in Ragtown. She had her answer. "Are you thinking about where you'll go next?"

"I'm not opposed to moving on," he said, "after the Kid is caught."

She'd hoped he would stay because she hoped for a day when people could walk the streets of Ragtown without fear of being gunned down. That day couldn't come until the criminal element was caught and put in prison. They needed a man who was good at the job.

"We need you for our sheriff," she said with sincerity.

The way he looked at her caused her poor heart to skip a beat.

"You'll get by with someone else."

"Is there a reason you don't settle down?"

"I can't say there is. That's just the long and short of it."

Rosamund despaired. Some men just couldn't stay in one place.

They reached the crowd who'd gathered in front of the Wells Fargo office. As Rosamund greeted her neighbors, Sheriff Kincaid leaned against a post and crossed his arms. She found his reluctance to socialize with the Ragtown brethren unsociable.

She returned to his side. "You don't make friends easily, do you?"

"If a man's law-abiding, I don't pay him much attention."

He took a gold watch out of his pocket and looked at the time. She saw initials engraved in the gold.

"A gift?" she asked.

"That's right."

"From your father?"

"Nope," he tucked the watch back in his vest pocket.

The watch piqued her interest. He'd at some point in his life received a gold watch from someone he'd known well, someone who cared about him.

She felt self-conscious, aware that he meant more to her than just any man standing there.

"I'm sorry," she said.

He arched an eyebrow. "For what?"

"For our differences," she said.

"You don't ever have to apologize for having an opinion."

"Even if I don't agree with you?"

He didn't get a chance to answer. The stagecoach rumbled down the main street, the driver hollering and whooping at the team of six horses. He pulled up in front of the Wells Fargo office. The dust made everyone turn away, coughing.

Rosamund held a handkerchief to her nose. Men jumped down from the back of the stage and brushed the trail dust off their clothes. Others unloaded the cases. Their oaths salted the air.

Rosamund wasn't offended as she would've been in Virginia. By all measures, these men were courageous and the service they provided to their community was incalculable. They braved the hot sun and windstorms that drove the dirt into their eyes and ears. They'd encountered dangerous highwaymen who'd take their life for a ship-

ment of gold. If they had a few choice words to say, that
was their prerogative.

The stagecoach driver jumped down from his seat.

"Any trouble?" Matthew asked him, stepping forward.

The man pulled down his dirt-encrusted bandana. "No,
sir but I heard talk that the Kid is back in Churchill
County."

Rosamund looked at Matthew. He handled the news
without any emotion showing on his face.

"Who told you this?" Matthew asked.

The driver spat on the ground. "Settlers over in Dayton. The Kid shot up the Mercantile and killed the owner
and his missus."

Rosamund's breath caught in her throat. Matthew had
been right. The Kid had killed again. With chilling
certainty, she knew his murderous rampage wouldn't end
until a lawman brought him in.

"Did you hear if he was alone?" Matthew asked.

"That's what they say. A lone gunman traveling this
way."

The pall of inevitable death settled over them.

A frantic murmur rose from the crowd and then a bar-
rage of questions. The stagecoach driver stepped up on to
the boardwalk to answer them.

Rosamund searched Matthew's face for a glimpse into
what he was thinking. His jaw was set and his eyes
narrowed.

There were other lawmen between here and Dayton,
she wanted to scream. Let them take care of the Kid. She
kept this opinion to herself. Matthew Kincaid wouldn't
shirk his duty, no matter what she said.

Rosamund heard sputtering and the unmistakable tone
of a woman complaining coming from inside the stage-

coach. The driver returned and opened the door. He reached inside. A lace-gloved hand grasped his and a lady descended the steps. She looked around her with a disapproving gaze bearing down on the assembly, then straightened out her voluminous skirts.

Rosamund sighed. Aunt Hester had arrived.

Hester shook out a fan and began fanning herself with a delicate instrument of whalebone and brightly colored silk. Her hat was a symphony of ostrich feathers, now crushed by their confinement inside the stagecoach. Her dress was beset by adornments the likes of which most of these settlers had never seen.

None of the finery was new and it showed signs of wear.

When Hester spotted Rosamund, she shut her fan and hastened toward her.

"Aunt Hester," Rosamund claimed her on the top step of the boardwalk.

"My dear Rosamund," Hester gushed.

They hugged and kissed as if they were on the veranda of her father's house in Richmond.

"You've come such a long way," Rosamund said.

"That I have, child and the journey has tired me." Hester pulled away. "I don't know how you manage in all this dirt."

"You look well."

"I will survive, I expect, but enough about me," Hester said, her hand fluttering. "Let me get a good look at you."

Rosamund managed a weak smile and braced herself for Hester's evaluation.

"Bless my word," Hester said, after given Rosamund a quick looking over. "You're as dark as a field hand."

She didn't give Rosamund time to reply. She turned on

Matthew. Her gaze landed on the seven-point star pinned to his vest.

"You must be the new sheriff," she said.

Aunt Hester had loved Jake. He'd been a Southern gentleman of the very best sort and had treated his Auntie like a duchess. When he'd taken the position of sheriff, she'd been as proud as all of the family had been.

"Let me introduce you," Rosamund said. "Matthew Kincaid, this is Aunt Hester Sherry."

Hester examined Matthew Kincaid as an interloper but she remembered her manners.

"Sheriff," Hester said, extending her gloved hand.

"Ma'am," he said with rakish charm.

Auntie's gaze cut him with razor sharp precision. He hadn't won her over.

Sheriff Kincaid looked about as out of place on a veranda as a man could be. He took Aunt Hester's hand and shook it vigorously.

"Well," Hester said, retrieving her hand from his grasp.

"Aunt Hester has traveled all the way from Richmond," Rosamund explained. His gaze shifted to Rosamund. She saw a hint of a smile.

"I hope your journey was agreeable," he said with positively touching good manners.

Aunt Hester recoiled as if she'd come in contact with a hot iron.

"You're a Yankee," she said, responding to his flat Northern accent.

"Yes, ma'am."

Hester looked at him in horror.

"Let's go along to my house," Rosamund took ahold of Hester's arm before there was a confrontation. Hester could be a formidable foe. "Jason will bring along your cases."

"Rosamund, how can this be?"

"I will explain when we are at the house."

Their sheriff put two fingers to the brim of his hat. Hester nodded with superior airs.

"Luckily the house isn't far." Rosamund steered her aunt in that direction.

"Yes, I could use a proper cup of tea." The fan came out.

"Make no mistake, that's a handsome woman just arrived on my stage."

Aunt Hester stiffened.

Rosamund shot a look of disapproval over her shoulder. The stagecoach driver rubbed his grizzled face as he watched them walk away. Matthew looked like he was about to burst out laughing. Instead, he winked at Rosamund.

"And Rosy is pretty, too," Matthew said.

Rosamund squelched a response. Auntie would never reply to such a public assessment of her virtues but Rosamund was close to a fit of giggles. Still, she returned Matthew's ungentlemanly comments with a haughty look of reproach.

She managed to navigate Hester down the boardwalk with as much *sang-froid* as she could muster.

A few minutes later, they stood in front of the two story timber framed house Jake had built.

It was meant to be a home.

"You didn't tell us that Jake's replacement was a Yankee," Hester said accusingly. "There wasn't time," Rosamund explained. "He's only just arrived."

"Don't expect me to be sociable with him."

"He's not the only person here from the North."

"Dear me, I had no idea Ragtown was such a disagreeable place."

"Auntie, we don't take sides here. This is a small town and we rely on each other no matter where that person's from originally. We aren't Northerners or Southerners anymore. I guess you could say we are Westerners."

Auntie pressed her lips together into a thin line. She was set in her ways. Her hatred ran deep and completely. She would never be persuaded that she didn't honor the dead by her hatred of the living.

"Please come in," Rosamund said.

Hester hesitated. The house was small by Virginia standards. "There isn't any veranda or even a front porch."

"We were going to add a porch when we had the money," she explained.

Hester didn't frown. She never frowned because she didn't want to encourage wrinkling, but Rosamund sensed her disappointment.

She opened the door and Auntie peered inside.

"There are four rooms downstairs. The upstairs isn't finished yet. I've made up one of the front rooms for you. I do hope you will be comfortable."

Hester stepped across the threshold. She removed her hat and gloves and handed them to Rosamund. "If my brother, General Sherry, could see how you are living, my dear girl, he'd be very disenchanted."

Rosamund didn't shrink from the criticism. She expected Aunt Hester's disapproval.

"I know this isn't what you are used to," Rosamund said, "but it's important to understand that out here we make do."

"That's apparent to me," Hester replied.

Rosamund didn't despair. Hopefully, Hester's stay would be a short one.

The feathers in Hester's hat tickled her nose and made Rosamund sneeze. She placed the hat and the pair of gloves on the hall chair. She noticed the gloves had been repaired with white thread, a different color from the creamy lace.

It was a deficiency that would've been commented on at all the homes in Richmond. Rosamund had no intention of embarrassing her auntie but she wondered what it meant. How had fashionable Aunt Hester allowed herself to be seen in such a shabby pair of gloves?

Rosamund removed her bonnet and patted a stray hair into place.

"Look at you," Hester said. "Your complexion is ruined and your hands are a disaster."

Rosamund looked at her hands. They were red from this morning's washing. "I've changed but so has our world."

"So you have said." Hester dismissed Rosamund's observations with a huff.

Hester checked her appearance in the hall mirror. She still wore the pin curls that were the vanity of her youth twenty years ago. Her complexion, though aged, still radiated the pampered lifestyle she grew up with.

"What is the name this new sheriff calls you?" Hester asked.

"Rosy," she replied.

"Sound vulgar to me. And way too familiar."

Rosamund was beginning to like the name. "The rest of the town calls me Mrs. Jake. You'll find people are less formal out here."

Hester turned to face her. The swish of her gown brought back happy memories of her childhood in

Rosamund.

"Formal or not, it isn't gentlemanly to abbreviate a lady's name."

Matthew Kincaid wasn't a gentleman, not in the traditional sense. Rosamund wasn't even sure what kind of man he was, although her intuition encouraged her to believe that he was a good man.

"You'll find most men in this town are well-mannered," she said defensively.

"Not from what I've observed."

Rosamund would say no more. She didn't want their reunion to begin in a quarrel. What Hester sought to remind Rosamund was the standard of propriety she'd been raised with. It was this standard their men had fought bravely to uphold. She felt guilty for having dismissed these standards so easily.

"If you would be so kind to show me to my room. I need to wash." Thankfully, Hester hadn't any more to say about the sheriff. "Have your girl bring me some hot water."

"I have no servants," Rosamund replied.

"Who takes care of you?" Hester spoke with disbelief.

"I take care of myself."

Hester sighed. "This is all too much. Now I am here and I will see that you are taken care of properly."

Rosamond kissed the woman on her powered cheek. Up close, her age showed through the cracks in the powder on her face. The skin around her eyes sagged into folds.

"I'm glad you are here as I am glad for your company. I will try to make your visit a happy one. I do hope you will be amenable to our hospitality."

Rosamund's words seemed to pacify the woman.

"Your room is here," Rosamond opened the door to

the room with a window to the street. It was her favorite because it was sunny most of the day. She'd sewn drapes lined with cotton so that Hester could sleep in as was her custom.

"I'll bring you some hot water," Rosamund said.

"That would be lovely."

Hester sank into the green parlor chair Rosamund had dragged into her room. Exhaustion felled her like a giant oak.

Rosamund hurried out of the stifling presence of her husband's aunt. Much as she appreciated company, she'd been independent long enough to resent her smothering ways.

The woman represented the old ways and a life that had long been left behind.

Rosamund didn't want Hester to be unhappy or forget the way Richmond had been before the War. She truly didn't. Hester had always been the proudest of ladies and there were many traditions in their past worth preserving.

Having Hester here would be more formidable a trial than Rosy—for that's how she wished to be called now—had anticipated. Inevitably, they would clash over Rosy's new life for Hester would never recognize Rosy's need to carve her own destiny out of this wilderness.

She brought the steaming kettle back to Hester's room. Hester had removed her pelisse. Rosy poured hot water into a ceramic basin, steaming up the oval mirror above.

"This isn't what you're used to," Rosy said, holding a sliver of soap, "but this is what we use out here."

Hester didn't take the soap. "I've brought my own."

Rosy nodded. She should've guessed. "I'll have tea ready in the parlor when you're ready. I want you to tell me all the news of Richmond."

Hester had no way of knowing but her starchy attitude had stiffened Rosy's resolve to stay in Ragtown. She kissed the lady again.

"I'm so glad you've come. We've a great deal to talk about." She left the room.

Chapter Four

"I SHOULD HAVE written," Aunt Hester said, sipping tea out of a dainty cup from Rosy's grandmother's Spode tea service. "I didn't know how to put ...things."

Rosy heard the pain in Hester's voice and feared the worse. "Are Mother and Father all right?"

"Perfectly. They send their best."

"What is it?" Rosy demanded to know.

Hester's bosom rose and fell. Her eyes moistened with tears.

"Tell me," Rosy said more gently for she'd no wish to add to Hester's obvious distress.

Hester put the cup and saucer down on the table. She pulled a handkerchief out from her sleeve and folded her hands in her lap. "My brother lost Daddy's farm. The bank foreclosed to pay his debts about six weeks ago. Every last stick of furniture was sold at auction. The livestock is gone. His prized Belgians sold for a song."

Rosy was devastated by this news. She was truly sorry for Hester. She'd lived at Seven Oaks all her life and was devoted to her brother, Jake's father, a Confederate general. The Sherrys were proud people who loved their land.

"This is devastating news," Rosy said truthfully.

Hester's face puckered as she dabbed at fresh tears with the frilly handkerchief. "It's been a blow to all of us but what choice did my brother have? All of his money was in Confederate bills."

Rosy knew it was the final humiliation of a loyal family.

"I had no idea. My mother gave no indication in her letter," Rosamond said.

"They didn't want you to know."

"I don't understand why?"

"We agreed to keep the news from you given how you'd suffered your own terrible loss." Hester looked away and buried her face in her handkerchief.

Rosy recognized her mother and father's hand in keeping this news from her. They'd always protected her and her siblings from the harshness of the real world. They wouldn't want to burden their recently widowed daughter with additional sadness.

The Sherrys had probably been too humiliated to put pen to paper.

"I can't tell you how sorry I am," Rosy said.

Hester sniffed. "It's been a terrible ordeal for everyone."

"Where did you go? Where do you live?"

"Brother and his wife moved into town."

This was Rosy's first clue of trouble ahead. Hester did not include herself in the relocation to Richmond.

"You don't know how bad it's gotten," Hester said. "The State of Virginia is run by Yankee carpetbaggers. They're a vile lot, Rosamund. Mark my words, they'll be the undoing of many a Southern gentleman and lady."

Hester's sobbed, her body shaking.

Rosy knelt before her aunt and wept. She wept for the past and she wept with compassion for all Auntie had lost. And she wept for a way of life that no longer existed.

"We must return to Richmond at once," Rosy said.

"That's impossible, my dear." Hester choked on the words.

"Why do you say so? I consider it my duty to return as soon as it can be arranged."

Hester cleared her throat. She hadn't told Rosy everything. Rosy braced herself for more bad news.

"It's not you who can't return but me."

Rosy was truly confused. "What are you talking about?"

Hester's gaze dropped to the floor, to the rough-sawn planks and the cotton rag rug. "You don't know what it feels like to be an extra mouth to feed, the useless maiden Auntie who everyone pities."

"Aunt Hester, don't say such things."

"I've been a burden all my life. And a nuisance."

Rosy began to protest but Hester stifled her with a raised hand.

"No need to be polite. I know who I am. My brother and his wife have stood their loss but they don't need me adding to their struggle."

"I'm so very sorry," Rosy said.

"War changes everything," Hester said. "Nothing for the better."

Rosy got to her feet and gave Hester a hug. Hester seemed restored by her affection.

"What will you do now?" Rosy asked, regaining her own composure.

"I'd hoped you'd let me stay here with you."

Rosy stared at Hester. The War had taken all Hester knew away from her but Auntie didn't want pity. No, pity was a waste. What Hester wanted was to be useful and that was all anyone could want, Rosy decided.

"You'll always have a home with me," Rosy said.

"Bless you, child. I'd hoped you let me stay."

"This is a good town. I can make a living as a teacher," Rosy said, drying her eyes with the back of her hand. "There's a garden and good water."

"I mean to do my share," Hester said. "Although I don't know what I'm good for except serving tea and idle gossip."

Rosy smiled. She didn't want Hester to worry but she had no idea the kind of life she'd be living.

"We've all learned this new way of life and you will as well. You'll be surprised at what you're capable of.

Hester squared her shoulders. "I suppose you're right. Enough tears have been shed. Life must go on."

Rosy was glad to hear her say so. Life would go on and they would be a family.

MORE TRUNKS AND cases arrived by freight from the railhead in Reno. Jason borrowed a handcart and lugged them to the house. True to his nature, he refused payment for his hard work.

Rosy looked at the luggage with dismay. She realized that Hester'd never had any intention of returning to Virginia.

Auntie had brought elaborate hats, silk shawls and expensive fans. And petticoats. There were yards and yards of starch-smelling petticoats, some trimmed with French ribbons, others adorned with Belgian lace. And whalebone corsets. Rosy had never seen such a collection of lady's undergarments.

Rosy held up a beautiful pair of green brocaded slippers. "Where do you expect to wear these?"

Hester looked forlorn. She loved her things and couldn't bear to part with any of them. Here in Ragtown, they had no purpose. There wouldn't be any fancy dress balls or elaborate tea parties. There wouldn't be any carriage rides through town in the waning hours of the day. To go calling on a neighbor dressed in such finery would be met with suspicion. Unknown to Hester, only the saloon women dressed up in silk and satin in the middle of the day.

"We shall sew you a practical dress from some of these cottons," Rosy said.

"Do you think that's necessary?"

"The women out here dress more modestly."

Hester nodded. "I do see your point. I do want to fit in."

Rosy was relieved that Hester was amenable to her suggestions. They repacked many of the garments and undergarments and settled them out of the way under Hester's bed.

She'd brought more than clothing. A toilet mirror of flame mahogany set on a mahogany vanity survived the journey, as did a crated bone china service for twelve. A collection of scent bottles arrived in green, red and amber.

When Rosy thought her house couldn't hold anymore, Jason and Adolph Bascomb arrived with the piano. The pair stood in her doorway, red-faced and sweaty.

"Is there anything you left in Richmond?" Rosy asked Hester.

Hester looked sheepish as well she might. "I know it was foolish of me and I do hope you won't be cross, but I couldn't leave my mother's piano behind."

Rosy wasn't cross. She was moved by her auntie's desperation to keep part of her past with her. She gestured for the man and the boy to bring the coffin shaped box into the parlor.

"Where do you want us to put this," Adolph said and he wiped his brow with his sleeve.

Rosy thought the east corner of the room would do just fine.

Adolph opened the crate with a crow-bar. Hester's face lit up as she watched her beloved piano lifted out and placed on its side. The legs had been removed for shipping and Hester hovered over Mr. Bascomb giving instructions as he pounded the piano legs into place.

Jason and Mr. Bascomb righted the instrument. It took up a great deal of space in the parlor.

When they'd finished, Hester beamed with pride. Rosy had to admit she liked the idea of having a piano in the house.

She offered the piano movers a glass of water.

Adolph shook his head. "Thank you, kindly but I best be getting back to the livery."

"Ma needs me to help at the store," Jason said and he followed Adolph out of the house.

Rosy and Hester stood in the parlor admiring the piano.

"Thank you, my dear," Hester said with tears in her eyes.

"Auntie, don't cry."

Hester swiped at the tears that had fallen on her plump cheek. "We shall be two roses among thorns, won't we Rosamund?"

Rosy grasped her hands. "Indeed we will."

Chapter Five

ROSY PAID A dollar for a fat rooster from Mr. Beaver at the livery. The man raised the best chickens in Churchill County and he boasted about the meatiness of his flock as he put the creature into a cage made of willow branches.

When it came to killing a chicken, Rosy was uncertain how to proceed. Mr. Beaver offered to behead it but Rosy declined with quiet confidence. If she was to become a pioneer woman, she needed to learn these everyday tasks.

She carried the rooster home and set the cage next to the stump Jake had used for a chopping block. His ax lay next to it.

Learning to cook on a wood-burning stove had been a challenge but dispatching a chicken proved to be more difficult than she'd imagined. The bird kept looking at her with a prideful expression and she began to feel sorry for him.

She opened the cage and the chicken flew out, cackling with indignation. He stood on top of the cage, looking around him with disdain.

Rosy took a length of rope from her apron pocket. "Come along," she said, reaching for him.

The chicken jumped off the crate and pecked on the ground. Rosy tried to grab him but the wily beast kept a few feet distance between them.

"You need some help?"

Rosy jumped.

Matthew Kincaid stood next to the shed, his arms crossed.

Rosy blotted her forehead with the back of her hand. "You startled me. How long have you been there?"

He smiled with male superiority. "Not long enough."

"I want to roast a chicken for diner but I'm not getting any cooperation from this rooster."

"You shouldn't have let him out of the cage," he said with authority.

"I understand that now. What can be done?"

Matthew uncrossed his arms. The rooster was about ten feet away. Matthew snuck up behind the bird and dove for him but the rooster was quicker. Both of them began running around the yard, the chicken protesting loudly.

Rosy began to laugh. Her laughter brought tears. She hadn't laughed in such a long while and it felt good.

The sheriff cornered the rooster behind the woodpile and threw a feed sack over its head. He grabbed his prey and carried him by the legs.

"He'll make a mighty fine meal," he said with a grin. He looked at her with a I-told-you-so expression on his face. To see him grinning delighted her beyond measure.

Rosy reached for the hapless bird. "Thank you, kindly. I don't think I would've ever caught him."

"I'll finish him off," Matthew said. He held the bird on the chopping block with his boot, stretched its neck and picked up the ax.

Rosy was going to be sick. She turned and started for the house when she heard the ax come down. The bird let out a loud squawk and then there was silence. She stood in the doorway, her back to Matthew, willing the queasiness to go away.

"He's ready to be plucked as soon as he's bled out," Matthew said behind her.

Rosy swallowed and turned. Her gaze flitted momentarily to the headless bird he held up by its feet, blood dripping on the ground.

"You all right?" he asked.

She met his gaze. She didn't want him to guess her condition. "I will be. This is a new experience for me."

Matthew nodded and handed her the rooster.

Holding the bird an arm's length away, she wanted to retch.

She smiled feebly as she looked up at Matthew. "What can I do for you? I assume you haven't come to help me with my chores?"

He patted his vest pocket and took out a piece of folded paper. "This came today by rider from the sheriff in Dayton."

He unfolded the paper and showed her. It was a poster showing a drawing of a man called the Kid. Across the top, the poster read, "Wanted. Dead or Alive."

"Is this the man who killed your husband?" Matthew asked.

Rosy recognized the youthful face. The artist had captured his likeness rather well. The poster offered a reward of two hundred dollars.

"Yes, I believe it is."

Matthew folded up the paper and put it back in his vest pocket. He looked so serious Rosy shuddered.

"He can no longer hide under the guise of anonymity, can he?"

"No, Rosy, he can't."

"That's a relief, I suppose. I wish we knew his name."

"We'll find out soon enough," he said with confidence.

"If you'll excuse me, I have work to do."

"Did I tell you fried chicken was my favorite?" he said.

"Why, Sheriff Kincaid, I don't believe you did."

"I reckon I'll see you later."

Rosy shook her head. He assumed correctly that the chicken was for him. "I suppose you will," she answered.

He was staring at her. There was no mistaking Matthew Kincaid's thoughts. She saw a deep yearning in his gaze. That kind of look sent shivers down her spine. She hoped he didn't notice. She didn't want to encourage him or give him any false notions.

"I'll be going," he said huskily.

She nodded and raised her chin.

He tipped his hat and departed, his spurs jingling in the stillness of the morning.

Rosy exhaled. The sheriff had a way of disrupting her equilibrium. She couldn't let him. She was still in black for heaven's sake and there was Hester to consider.

She held up the bird. The body still radiated warmth but the smell left her feeling queasy. She wrinkled her nose and headed for her kitchen.

HESTER CAME INTO the kitchen looking like a hound on a scent. "I didn't know you could cook."

Rosy took no offense. "I've learned to do many new things since coming to Ragtown."

"I do declare. You have changed."

"I'm told my cooking is good," she said.

Hester sniffed the air. "I must say whatever you're cooking does smell delicious."

Rosy used a dishtowel to lift the lid and show her the chicken bubbling in the cast-iron pan. The condensation dripped off the lid into the pan causing the grease to pop and sizzle.

"You've made more than enough," Auntie said.

Rosy replaced the lid. "This isn't all for us. I'm taking the sheriff his noon meal."

Hester's hand fluttered to her bosom and she collapsed into one of the kitchen chairs. "Really, Rosamund. How could you?"

Rosy felt her temperature rising. "Auntie, don't carry on so."

"You're consorting with the enemy. You dishonor the family name."

"I'm doing no such thing," Rosy said firmly. "I'm feeding a hungry man who is here to protect us."

Hester looked wounded. Rosy patted her shoulder. Hester had suffered greatly and the cost had been devastating.

"I'm sure this is an adjustment for you. Do be brave and try to understand. I wouldn't do anything to harm the Sherrys or you, but I'm tired of hating and I think the town would be better served if we bury our differences."

Rosy realized what she'd said. It was important to bury their differences. The morning Hester had arrived, she'd believed differences mattered but they didn't. Not in this new time and place.

Hester rose heavily from her chair and went to her room. There would be time for reconciliation later. Auntie would be difficult to convince. She clung to a past that no longer existed.

Rosy hurried to finish the cooking. She wanted to tell Matthew these things and more. She wanted him to know how important he was to her.

She carried the heavy basket outside to her wagon. The sun bore down with its midsummer heat and she'd neglected to put on her bonnet.

She pulled the wagon down the street. A freight wagon passed by but she didn't recognize the driver. The wagon carried a full load with a canvas tied over the top. The town was growing and so were its needs. Soon there would be a fine new school built for the children of Ragtown. She was ready to get started.

She was uneasy about the Kid being close by. Dayton was only a day's ride away. The sheriff there had warned Matthew the Kid might be heading their way. He was no longer anonymous. They'd be able to identify him from the poster. Everyone in town would be uneasy.

To her dismay, Matthew's horse was saddled and tied to the hitching post outside his office. She used her hip to push her way inside and saw him at the big oak desk loading his revolver. A handful of bullets was splayed out on the desk. She shuddered to see them as she set the basket down. They were a grim reminder of his deadly profession.

He looked up and smiled. His smile didn't calm the fear taking over her body.

"What do you have there?" he asked as if he didn't know.

"Why Sheriff, you know perfectly well I fried up that chicken you killed."

His smile broadened. It was his way of acknowledging his gratitude.

She uncovered the plate of chicken. "I do hope you like it."

Matthew loaded the last bullet into the gun's chamber.

She set the plate in front of him.

He shucked his weapon in its holster. "I must admit I've got an appetite."

She didn't reply because she didn't want him to guess how much she worried. She'd wait for him to finish his dinner before she beset him with questions.

While he ate, she went to the window. A group of four wranglers rode by. Adolph Bascomb sat out in front of the stage agent's office napping, his hat shading his face.

Mathew was taking his sweet time with his meal.

She sighed.

"What's on you mind, Rosy?"

"Have you heard anymore about the Kid?" she asked, her patience used up.

"No more than the wanted poster let on," he said between bites.

"Do you think he'll come around here?"

Mathew shrugged. "He could be anywhere. There are plenty of places to hide out between here and Dayton."

"Why's your horse saddled?" She turned to face him.

He smacked his lips. "I thought I'd take a ride out to the Rocking J."

"Is there a problem?"

"No, Rosy but I should get familiar with my surroundings."

"In case there's trouble."

"There's gonna be trouble." He licked off his fingers as casually as you please. "Your aunt settled in?"

"She is. Thank you for asking." Rosy chewed her lower lip. "She's decided to stay in Ragtown."

"You don't sound too happy about it."

"I don't?" Rosy sat down in the chair. "I don't mean to sound unhappy. I do want her here."

"Let me guess. She's a lady who's never known hard-ship."

"Sir, we Southern ladies have known plenty of hard-ship. We prefer not to show it."

Her rebuff didn't bring a response. Either he was being deliberately insensitive or he was more thick-headed than she'd imagined. She guessed the first. He liked to goad her. She couldn't think of a reason why.

"I thought your aunt came to take you home?"

"My home is here."

He picked up a chicken leg. The man could pack in a meal. "You ladies are going to be in dire straights come winter."

Rosy had never spent the winter in Ragtown. She'd never experienced cold weather before.

"I intend to earn some money. The town asked me to teach the children and I agreed."

"There're other ladies who could take the job."

She hated the doubt in his voice. "I'm equal to the task, I assure you."

He finished the leg in three bites and picked up another piece. "Where are you going to have this school?"

"The church will have to do for a start. The town is growing and a proper schoolhouse would be an important asset."

"Seems to me that'll cost."

"Mr. Turner has donated a parcel of land. As for mon-ey, I've a few ideas about raising funds for a school."

"I guess you've got this school all figured out."

She was glad to see he wiped his mouth off on the linen serviette she'd provided. "I have."

His eyes sparkled with amusement. "Rosy, you're quite a gal."

Blushing with genuine emotion, she handed him a clean serviette. Their hands touched. She made no move to withdraw her hand, nor did he.

Rosy had thought she was immune to a man's touch but the unmistakable longing to be with him overcame her like a fever. She could see the same longing in his gaze.

She leaned closer and held her breath in anticipation. What was she doing? She couldn't be with him. He was headed for a gunfight. He would kill or be killed. She couldn't risk her heart being broken again.

She straightened and pulled her scorched hand away. Had Mathew noticed her distress? Of course he had. She should say something, but no words were adequate to express her feelings.

Jason burst into the office with his usual energy. He carried his father's Winchester.

"You riding out?" he asked Matthew.

"As soon as I'm done with my feed."

"Can I go with you?" Jason's face glowed with adoration. Rosy's heart ached to see his enthusiasm.

"No," Matthew replied firmly.

"Aw, why not?" Jason's expression tightened.

"'Cause I say so."

"I'm real good with a gun," Jason said. "I've been practicing shooting at bottles set up on an old cottonwood down by the Carson River."

"You're a boy," Matthew replied coldly.

"I aim to be sheriff of this town one day," Jason said.

Matthew shot a look at Rosy. "In the meantime, you belong in school."

"There ain't no school, Sheriff Kincaid."

"There's gonna be," Matthew bellowed.

Jason bowed his head.

Rosy put her hand on Jason's shoulder. "Maybe you can ride with the sheriff another time."

She waited for confirmation from Matthew but he ignored the boy's misery. He stood up and buckled on his gun belt.

He wasn't about to put Jason in harm's way and Rosy silently thanked him for it. Despite his gruff manner, he was protective of her, Jason and every other citizen in their community.

She could love this man.

"Come on," she said to the boy. "You can accompany me to the Mercantile."

She looked back at Matthew. He scowled as he finished getting ready. He'd retreated to a dark place. She wondered why. Who didn't protect you when you were a boy, she wanted to ask him. Who forgot to look out for young Matthew Kincaid?

Chapter Six

ROSY HADN'T EXAGGERATED when she said she had a plan to raise funds for the school. The very next morning, she put her plan into working order. There was one business in town that always seemed to have an abundance of cash and Rosy intended to pay the patrons a visit.

She pushed through the batwing doors of the Easy saloon.

"Good morning, gentleman."

Heads came up from card games. The bartender stopped pouring a round of drinks.

"As you know, my name is Mrs. Sherry," she said in her sweet Southern drawl. "Jake Sherry was my husband."

She heard a soft murmur of voices.

"I've taken on the position of schoolteacher for Ragtown. I need your help."

The men stared at her with their mouths open. She'd decided against her black dress and worn her Sunday best dress instead. Hester had let her borrow one of her elaborately decorated hats. She'd dabbed a bit of rouge on her cheeks, although not enough to compete with the saloon dollies. A splash of camellia-scented perfume drove home the point that she was here to conduct business but hadn't sacrificed her femininity to do so.

"Mr. Turner has generously donated an acre of land,"

she continued, building her case. "We need your help financing the lumber for putting up a building."

"I don't know if a school is necessary," the bartender said. "I never had any book learning and it didn't hurt me none."

The other men nodded in agreement.

A saloon dolly descended the stairs. She sashayed up to Rosy, pulled up her skirt, revealing a moth-holed stocking and took out a silver dollar from her garter.

"Here, Mrs. Sherry, this is all I got but I want the children of this town to have a school."

Rosy smiled with gratitude and took the money. "Thank you for your contribution. Please call me Rosy."

"All right, Rosy," the woman said. Her front teeth were missing but otherwise she had a beautiful smile. "My name is Big Nellie."

Big Nellie put her hands on her hips and challenged the men with a meaningful look.

Rosy untied her fancy hat and pulled it off as if she meant to stay. The men looked uncomfortable. She circled the table and the men hunched over their pile of winnings.

Big Nellie started to laugh. The sound came from deep inside her with a richness Rosy liked hearing.

"Levi, how 'bout you?" Big Nellie said to the bartender. "What call you got for all your dough? You got no family to provide for. The children of this town need a school, so ante up."

The man frowned but he pulled a five-dollar gold piece out of his vest pocket and laid it on the bar.

"There you go, honey. That's Levi being generous, the likes of which none of us have ever seen before."

The other men laughed but tepidly. Levi didn't even pretend to be happy about giving away so much money.

Rosy thanked him warmly and placed the coin in her hat. She passed her hat around again. Each man dropped a few coins inside.

"This is good for a start," she said enthusiastically after every one of them had contributed. "You all are certainly to be commended for caring about the future of our town."

The men stopped their moping. Big Nellie slapped her thigh and laughed. Her laugh came straight from her belly.

"Thank you for your help," Rosy said to her. "Thank you all."

"You're more than welcome," Big Nellie replied. "You come back and visit with us any old time."

Levi didn't share in her offer of hospitality. The men returned to their cards.

Rosy wasn't finished. "I hope," she said with a flourish of her gloved hand, "that I can count on all of you to help build the school."

She left them with the request. She'd no doubt they'd all roll up their sleeves and put up a fine-looking building. When they finished, Ragtown would have its very own schoolhouse.

Rosy turned for the sheriff's office to show Matthew what she'd accomplished at the saloon. He'd never guess that she'd gone into the saloon alone or ask for help from strangers. She wanted him to know she had the backbone to be a pioneer woman. Most importantly, she wanted him to know she wasn't Rosamund anymore, she was Rosy.

TWO MEN CAME out of the Wells Fargo office pushing Adolph Bascomb in front of them. They laughed and joshed but the sound was mean and cruel. Both men began punching Adolph. The poor man covered his head with his hands but the blows knocked him sideways. He fell backward off the boardwalk.

The two men kept after him. The bigger man shoved Adolph and kicked dirt in his face. His partner roared with laughter.

"Those men are drunk again," Alice Turner said as she beckoned Rosy to come inside the Mercantile.

Rosy hurried through the door. The two women huddled in front of the window watching Adolph take the beating the men hurled at him. At last, Adolph cried out. Rosy couldn't bear to see Adolph so defenseless.

"We should do something," Rosy said.

"Nothing we can do," Alice replied. "There's too many."

Those men didn't seem to notice Matthew Kincaid exiting the sheriff's office and heading their way. Rosy rallied. No one would get away with such disgusting behavior with the lawman around.

When Matthew reached them, he grabbed both men by the collars.

They tried to spin around but the sheriff held them steady. When their hands went to their gun holsters, Matthew knocked their heads together.

The men crumbled into a heap in the dust.

Matthew helped Adolph to his feet. Adolph picked up his hat, shaking.

A crowd gathered quickly and several men helped Matthew drag the unconscious ruffians to the jail.

Alice turned away from the window. "Our sheriff taught those boys a lesson they'll not soon forget."

"Maybe I should go and fetch Dr. McKinnon?"

"Don't bother the old doc. Those two will have mighty big headaches when they come around but they'll live."

Adolph walked unsteadily but looked capable of getting himself back to work at the livery.

Rosy struggled with mixed emotions at what she'd seen. She admired Matthew's decisive action. Adolph was too old and crippled with arthritis to have put up a fight and those ruffians clearly took advantage.

On the other hand, Matthew had used force instead of negotiations to stop the behavior. Rosy felt strongly that words were mightier than fists.

"I wish he hadn't needed to hurt those men."

"Come now," Alice said. "You're way too tenderhearted."

"I suppose that's true but the town will never be tamed until we stop using violence."

"That's everybody's wish," Alice replied. "Still, the new sheriff did get the job done."

Rosy wasn't surprised by Alice's response. Everybody in Ragtown was of the same opinion. She knew she'd been sheltered by loving parents and a husband from the evil that men do. If she was going to live in this restless land, she would have to prepare herself for the inevitability of the things she hated most.

Matthew had tried to tell her so time and time again. In his world, justice was swift. Violence begat violence. Rosy was firm in her conviction that there was a better way to handle crime in their town.

"I was on my way to the sheriff's office," Rosy said. "Do you think it's safe to go there?"

"Don't you worry. Those two are locked up and won't be bothering nobody for a long while."

Rosy left her donations with Alice and put on her hat.

With thanks and a goodbye, she went outside. The crowd had dispersed and went about their business.

She walked across the street and waved at Will Cannon who'd pushed open the door of the barbershop. He didn't linger for a few words of conversation and hurried in the other direction.

His retreat saddened her. Will had been avoiding her since Jake's death and the Kid's escape. She knew he blamed himself for what'd happened and was too embarrassed to talk to her.

Rosy resolved to pay a call on him soon. She wanted him to know she didn't hold any bad feelings toward him. Nobody should have to carry around an abundance of guilt. Who could've predicted that a man who'd been caught stealing a horse would turn out to be a murderer?

Rosy entered the sheriff's office and saw, to her relief, the two prisoners awake and sitting on the floor of the cell rubbing their heads.

Matthew had buckled on his holster and was tying it around his leg with a strip of rawhide.

"Morning, Rosy," he said.

"Good morning, Sheriff," she said in deference to the prisoners.

She leaned forward so she could speak in a whisper. "Did you have to conk them so hard?"

"Those boys needed to be taught some manners," he replied for all to hear.

She straightened. "I'm glad we are in agreement about their poor conduct, it's the method of arresting them we disagree about."

He finished and shucked the revolver in its holster. "Rosy, don't come in here and tell me how to do my job."

Rosy was hurt. "I was only speaking my mind."

"You're all gussied up and smell like summer flowers. Seems to me you mean to have your way."

Rosy couldn't believe the man's high opinion of himself. With complete disregard for the prisoners who were no doubt listening, Rosy gave as good as she got. "So you think I've put on perfume and wore my best dress for you?"

He gave her a crooked smile.

"Think what you like," she said. "I came to tell you I've been to the saloon."

His smile turned into a grimace. "You don't say."

"I do say and my visit was very lucrative."

"Come again?"

"Profitable. The patrons of that establishment provided me funds for building a schoolhouse."

"They gave you their cash?" Matthew whistled and shook his head.

"Every last one of them."

"You are something," he said. "You have a heap of determination for a little gal."

Rosy beamed with satisfaction. She'd met this challenge with a satisfactory result and Matthew acknowledged her in a way he hadn't before. She had the distinct impression that she'd gained his respect.

"There are different ways of getting a job done," she reminded him.

He picked up his hat. "I'd avoid that saloon. A lady don't belong there."

"I'll keep your advice under consideration."

They were at a stalemate again. He wanted to protect her from danger but he couldn't every hour of the day. She had to face her own challenges. If she didn't, she'd never last out here in this dangerous land.

"Where are you going?" she asked.

"Had word from a freighter just arrived that the Kid killed a settler and his wife up north just a few days ago."

"How awful."

His gaze held hers. If there was something she could say to stop him from going, she would.

She stepped closer. "Wouldn't it be better to enlist the aid of the sheriff up in Virginia City? Send a telegram, for goodness sake, so he will join you?"

"Can't. The lines are down and it could be days before the telegraph is operating again." He smiled a heart-stopping smile. "You don't have to worry about me. If that varmint's headed up to Virginia City, I'll rustle up the sheriff and a posse if need be to find him."

"Who's going to protect us if the Kid decides to ride into town while you're away?" She tried to keep the panic out of her voice.

He considered her question. "Will Cannon is more than able to defend this town."

"I suppose that's true but isn't your duty to stay here?"

He reached for her hand. His touch sent summer heat through every inch of her.

"You know I've got a job to do. The Kid is wanted in Ragtown and I'm going to bring him in."

Rosy stepped out of his reach. Obviously, nothing she said would deter him. She hated that she was afraid. She hated that he might not come back.

"What's got you all riled?" he asked.

She looked up into his eyes. "I don't know what I'd do if you were killed."

He punched the crown of his hat and then shaped a dent with the side of his hand. "I'll be all right," he said. "Don't you fret."

He put on his hat and bid her farewell.

Rosy didn't go to the doorway to wave him off. She heard his horse nicker and then men talking. The town expected him to do his job and he was a man sworn to do his duty.

She'd wanted him to hold her and reassure her that everything would be all right. He hadn't. She knew better than anyone that there were no guarantees he would come back to her.

Chapter Seven

A UNT HESTER SAT in the parlor working on a cross-stitch sampler. She wore a rose-colored tea gown embroidered with blue flowers and a tortoiseshell comb in her hair. Her experienced fingers dove into the stretched fabric with the nimbleness of a girl of twenty. She was the picture of quiet domesticity, and, Rosy hoped, contentment.

Rosy shut the front door behind her.

"How did the fund-raising go?" Hester asked, without looking up.

"Amazingly well," Rosy replied as she removed her hat.

"There's hot water ready if you want some tea."

"That sounds wonderful. I'll make a pot but first we need to talk."

Hester stopped and lifted her gaze. Her expression showed genuine alarm.

Rosy regretted the sharpness of her tone but since Matthew's departure, she'd been disconsolate. She'd admitted to herself that she'd fallen in love.

She was certain he loved her.

She'd thought a lot about how empty he'd looked when he first jumped down from the stagecoach. And how surprised he'd been when she'd brought him a hot meal and how he'd wanted to kiss her. How could she forget the incident with the rooster? Oh, yes, she'd seen the desire in his eyes.

Rosy could've made him happy if only she'd had the chance. It was too late. He'd gone after the outlaw. The likelihood of him surviving a shootout and returning to her was far from certain.

"I need to tell you something," Rosy said.

Hester started to speak but Rosy raised her hand to silence her. She'd never been abrupt with Auntie, but she needed the woman to listen.

"I loved Jake, you know I did. A part of me always will. I've come to love this little town and its future."

"My dear, do sit down and tell me what's put you in such a state?" Hester put her sampler on the table and folded her hands in her lap.

Rosy sat down in a straight back chair, the one that was the least comfortable in the room.

"You noticed I'm not wearing black anymore," she said.

"Do you think that's wise?" Hester replied. "It's only been three months."

"I can't mourn anymore."

"What will people say?" Hester cautioned.

"I hope they'll say that life continues. That there's a great deal of work to be done."

Hester didn't reply.

"There's another reason I'm shedding black, the best of reasons. I'm carrying Jake's baby."

Hester gasped. "You're sure?"

"Positive."

"Oh dear, think I'm going to faint," Hester cried.

Rosy wasn't prepared for this response.

Hester's head fell back. "Water, Rosamund. Do bring

me something to drink."

Alarmed, Rosy hurried to the kitchen and poured a glass of water from the ceramic jug. By the time she returned, Hester was fanning herself with both hands.

She pressed the glass to her lips.

Hester sputtered and coughed. She recovered but looked confused as if she didn't recognize her surroundings.

Her shuttered gaze fell on Rosy. "A baby? Are you certain?"

"Very certain." Rosy placed the glass on the table and took her hand. Her skin was as cold as ice.

"General Sherry will bellow like a mad bull when he finds out. He'll want you in Richmond straightaway."

"I know but I'm staying here."

"He'll insist."

"How could I go and leave you here by yourself?"

Hester's expression softened. "How will we manage?"

"We will have to rely on each other."

The handkerchief came out of the sleeve. Hester dabbed at the corners of her eyes.

Rosy let the moment settle. They'd spoken honestly to each other, maybe for the first time.

Hester regained her composure she looked up at Rosy. "I'll try my best."

Rosy hugged the woman around the neck. "Thank you, Auntie."

"Rosamund Sherry, you're going to make me cry." She didn't cry.

When Rosamund broke away, Hester picked up her sampler. She seemed truly happy for the first time since she'd arrived.

MATTHEW DIDN'T COME home that day or the next. Rosie's concern only intensified when nobody in town, not even Will Cannon, heard from him. Those who arrived from the northern routes were questioned but nobody had seen him or the Kid.

Rosy began to wonder if Mathew had received wrong information or worse, that the Kid had set up a trap.

When the telegraph lines were fixed, she sent a telegram to the sheriff in Virginia City. He'd replied that Sheriff Kincaid hadn't been through his town and he hadn't come across the outlaw called the Kid.

Her thoughts were heavy with gunfights and ambushes, of killing and bloody bullet holes the size of Liberty dimes. What if Mathew had been injured in a shoot-out and left for dead? What if he had died?

Even Hester noticed and when she asked Rosy what was wrong, Rosy confessed: Love had found her again.

"With the Yankee sheriff?" Hester said, sputtering.

Rosy nodded.

"Rosamund, he's not our kind."

"He's a good man," Rosy replied. "He's gone after Jake's killer."

Hester looked at her with unexpected sympathy in her gaze before collapsing into the nearest chair. She bowed her head.

Rosy feared she'd made a mistake telling her aunt.

"When I was you age," Hester said, her gaze far away, "I held on to my youth, refusing suitor after suitor. It was a game I was good at playing. There were many fine men who came to Daddy's door. I even liked one or two. I was looking for perfection. What a silly notion." Hester straightened. "Look at me now. I depend on my nephew's widowed wife to take me in."

"There's still plenty of time to marry if that's what you want," Rosy replied.

Hester shook her head. "I waited too long. I played the game too well."

"I'm sorry," Rosy said sincerely.

"I can't say I approve of your choice," Hester said, "but I will try to be civil with this man."

"Auntie, I'm so glad you approve."

"The child must have a father."

Rosy believed Matthew Kincaid would make an excellent father. She prayed that he would return so she could tell him.

ROSY BUSIED HERSELF with directing the building of the schoolhouse. There were plenty of volunteers. Seasoned lumber arrived from Virginia City and the post and beam structure went up quickly. A week later, the schoolhouse was finished.

The entire town assembled in the front of the one-room building to admire what they'd built. There were congratulations all around and promises that the children would be sent.

Rosy understood her purpose. She'd earned her right to stay in Ragtown.

Hester prepared the noonday meal as Rosy paced the floor.

"It's been ten days," she said.

"Sit down, my dear. Some hot chicken soup will do you and that baby a world of good."

Rosy was too nervous to sit. "I'll take some soup down to Will. Surely, he's had some word from Matthew."

"If you think that's best," Hester replied in a tone that left no doubt she didn't approve. Hester still clung to the old ways of courtship although she was trying to change.

"I do," Rosy said.

Hester didn't argue. She set about helping Rosy prepare the basket with leftover bacon and cornbread.

Rosy heard a knock at the door.

"Who could that be?" she asked, barely able to contain her excitement.

"You'd better go find out," Hester replied.

Rosy flew out of the room and flung open the door.

Angus McFarland stood there with a bunch of sage-brush clutched in his outstretched hand. He'd bathed and the few strands of hair on his head had been combed across his forehead.

Rosy was disappointed but hid it. She gave the man a welcoming smile. "Why, Mr. McFarland, how good of you to call."

He looked past Rosy into the parlor. "Is your aunt home?"

"I believe she is. Won't you come in?"

"Most obliged," he said nervously and he stepped inside. He shifted his feet as Rosy shut the door.

"Do sit down and I will tell Aunt Hester that you're here."

He sat in the nearest chair and set his hat on his knee.

Rosy stifled a giggle as she returned to the kitchen.

"Who was that at the door?" Hester asked as she stirred the soup pot.

"I do believe you have a gentleman caller," Rosy replied.

Hester's eyes widened. "Tell me who it is."

"Mr. McFarland."

Hester reddened, looking close to apoplexy. "That horrid stagecoach driver?"

"He brought you flowers," Rosy told her with a straight face.

Hester waved the wooden spoon. "Send him away at once."

"That would be rude."

Hester handed her the spoon. "I shall do it myself then."

The woman hurried off but Rosy saw her check her appearance in the hall mirror.

Rosy shook her head. No doubt Hester would sacrifice her own happiness for Rosy and her baby. Rosy couldn't let her do that. She intended to give cupid a little nudge and Auntie wouldn't be the wiser.

She finished packing the basket and added two extra plates for the prisoners. She hefted the basket outside to her wagon.

The wind carried a fair amount of grit this morning. Rosy bowed her head and started pulling the wagon down the street.

Will Cannon was about the same age that she was. He was shorter than Matthew but sturdily built. He hadn't been able to look Rosy in the eye since Jake died. Rosy wished she could put Will's mind at ease. Maybe some of Hester's cornbread would persuade him.

As she entered the sheriff's office, Will and Barney Nivens, a man of all trades, scrambled to their feet. They were playing checkers on the big oak desk.

Rosy smiled. No matter how rough and uncivilized Ragtown could be at times, the men did try to show some semblance of good manners when a lady was present.

Will studied the top of the desk.

"Hello, Will, Barney," she said.

"If you're looking for the sheriff," Will said, "he's not back yet."

"Yes, I know." She rested the basket on the edge of the desk.

"He'll be back before long," Barney said.

Rosy's pulse quickened. "Have you had word?"

Will shook his head. "No, ma'am. Don't you fret. He knows what he's doing."

"Don't you go worrying about Matthew," Barney said. "That boy can take care of himself. He's a crack shot by all accounts and good at tracking."

She felt deflated despite these reassurances. All she did lately was worry.

"I sent a telegram to the sheriff in Virginia City but he hasn't seen Matthew," Rosy unpacked the basket. "You don't suppose he could use some help?"

"The sheriff told me to watch these prisoners, so I can't leave," Will replied.

"He means to bring the Kid in," Barney added. "He's not the type to rest until he does what he sets out to do."

She tried to set her mind at ease but the frontier was unforgiving and the Kid was cunning. Matthew would have to keep his wits about him to survive.

"Do I smell cornbread?" Barney asked, rubbing his hands together.

"Yes, you do," she replied. "I brought you boys some dinner."

"That's nice of you Mrs. Jake, ain't it Will?" Barney said.

Both men's gazes traveled to her basket but she saw a

flicker of regret on Will's face.

It didn't take long for those two to clear their game of checkers off the desk. Rosy removed one of the white serviettes and spread it out for a tablecloth.

"I don't mind telling you I haven't et a proper meal since the sheriff left," Barney said. He elbowed Will in the arm.

"How about some of that grub?" one of the prisoners asked.

Rosy looked behind her. After a week behind bars, the two prisoners looked properly contrite for what they'd done to Adolph Bascomb.

"Seems to me this fare is too good for those boys," Barney said.

"I think they have learned their lesson," Rosy replied.

"We sure have, ma'am," one of the men said.

She put strips of bacon and a piece of cornbread onto one of her china plates and carried the plate over to the cell.

"Thank you, kindly, ma'am," they said in unison.

She slid the plate under the bars. "Sorry, you're going to have to share a plate. I only brought three."

The two men didn't seem to mind. They grabbed the food off the plate and shoved it into their mouths.

Rosy sat down in the oak chair and watched Barney and Will eat. They smacked their lips in appreciation of the meal and she found satisfaction in feeding their hearty appetites.

Mending her friendship with Will would take time but they'd made progress this morning. She hadn't realized what a serious young man he was.

The lack of news frustrated her. Where could Matthew be?

She jumped when she heard shouting in the street. Will pushed away from the table and took his gun out of its holster. All three of them rushed to the window.

"Now isn't that a sight for sore eyes," Barney said.

Walking down the main street was Sheriff Kincaid leading a dun horse. A young man was hogtied and draped across the saddle. Matthew's stocking-footed bay followed behind. Both horses had been ridden hard and their heads drooped. Their legs were covered in dried mud.

Rosy caught her breath. She recognized the prisoner. Matt had captured the Kid as he said he would and the Kid was alive.

Will pulled his serviette out of his shirt collar. "Don't that beat all."

"I told you," Barney said. He opened the door and stepped outside. Rosy was right behind him. Her heart beat wildly and she wasn't ashamed to show her delight in the return of the sheriff.

Without a word to the gathering crowd, Matthew tied the horses to the hitching rail in front of the jail. His dark beard made him look dangerous and he walked stiffly around the back of the horses.

The crowd pressed closer to get a good look at the Kid.

"Stay back," Matthew said. "This man is as mean as a rattler."

The people of Ragtown cleared a perimeter around the front of the jail but their curiosity about the Kid kept them inching closer.

Matthew drew his six-shooter. Will held his on the prisoner. Barney went back inside the jail and came out holding a rifle. He pointed it at the Kid's head.

Matthew grabbed the Kid by the belt and pulled him off the horse. The outlaw dropped to the ground. He sat up and smiled. His hands were shackled by steel handcuffs and his legs bound by iron. Matthew pulled him to his feet.

Rosy shuddered as the Kid looked around him, clearly amused by their curiosity. He'd killed five people that they knew about and would have probably killed again, Rosy reflected. Now he was finished and the law would deal with him.

Barney and Will stepped in closer in case the Kid had any ideas about escaping.

Matthew pushed the outlaw toward the open door.

The Kid shuffled up to the boardwalk. He saw Rosy and scanned her from head to the buttons on her shoes. Rosy didn't let his poor manners upset her. She met his gaze and kept her composure. She wanted him to know she wasn't afraid of him.

"Is this the man you saw your husband arrest for the thief of Lazarus Beaver's gelding?" Matthew asked.

She nodded.

"Move along," Matthew said to the Kid.

Matthew's eyes were red-rimmed and ready for sleep but his gaze reassured her he was glad to see her. They'd quarreled before he left and she deeply regretted what she'd said. As soon as this was over, she would tell him. She'd tell him how she'd held back loving him for no good reason. She would tell him how much she needed him.

The Kid stepped up on the boardwalk, the heavy shackles rattling.

Matthew asked Jason to throw down the saddlebags and take the mounts over to the livery.

Will guided the prisoner into the jail using the barrel of his gun. Jason led the two horses away. Barney picked up the bags and they followed Will inside, Rosy at his heels.

"You boys are taking up valuable room," Matthew

said to the two prisoners in the cell. They grabbed their hats and looked eager to go.

Matthew unlocked the door.

"Don't let me see you bothering anybody in this town again," he growled.

The two men bobbed their heads and promised the sheriff that they'd be model citizens from here on out. One of them picked up their plate off the floor and thanked Rosy for the meal. He handed her the plate and exited in a hurry.

Matthew paid them no mind and held the cell door open for the Kid. The prisoner sauntered into the cell as if he didn't have a care in the world.

With the prisoner locked up, Matt fell into the nearest chair and rubbed his eyes. He looked exhausted.

"Where'd you find him, Sheriff?" Barney dropped the saddlebag on the desk. Matthew undid the strap. "He was holed up in a homestead this side of Soda Lakes."

"Leave any survivors?" Barney asked.

"I buried a man, his woman and a young 'un."

Rosy felt sick. She reached for the back of a chair to steady herself. Matthew pulled a weapon out of the saddlebag and looked up at her. "Is this Jake's gun?"

She tore her gaze from him. She recognized the distinctive markings of the double-barrel weapon and her father-in-law's initials GS for Gunnison Sherry engraved in the barrel.

"Yes," she said, trembling.

"We've got our case," he said to the men. "Barney, send a telegram off to Carson for the judge."

Rosy started to pack up the men's empty plates. She didn't have an extra one but there was some cornbread left in the pan. She pushed the pan of food underneath

Mathew's chin. Their sheriff was home and needed something to eat.

The prisoner was holding on to the bars of his cell. He was very young. His complexion was bad and his teeth crooked. He beseeched her with an earnest look. Surprisingly, she didn't feel hatred for him. She thought she would. She did feel pity and believed strongly that he should be shown mercy.

She took out an extra piece of cornbread and wrapped it in a serviette. She handed the food to Will.

Will dropped the square of cornbread on the floor and kicked it. The Kid scooped it up and dove into the cornbread like he hadn't eaten in days. He finished quickly.

"Beg your pardon, ma'am," he said.

"Shut up," Matthew said, his mouth full.

"I wonder if you could do me a kindness?"

"Leave him be," Matthew told her. "He's a cold-blooded killer and can't be trusted."

"He's in a cell with his hands and feet bound up," she replied. "He can't do me any harm."

Matthew's expression turned to granite.

She looked back at the Kid. His smile was humble in contrast to the boldness she'd witnessed outside. "There's nothing I can do for you," she said kindly.

"I got a ma back East. I never learned to read or write. Could you take down a letter for her? Let her know what happened to the likes of her boy?"

"I could do that for you," she said.

"No, you won't." Matthew bellowed and rose to his feet so suddenly his chair toppled over.

"I think I need to," she said. She saw her civilized treatment of the Kid as a way of healing. "What harm could a letter do?"

Matthew's nostrils flared. "Did you hear what I said?"

"Of course I did, you spoke loudly enough for the entire town to hear," she replied.

He slammed his fist on the desk. "It's time for you to leave. Will, escort the lady out of here."

Rosy met Will's advance with prickly scorn. He had the good sense to back away.

"I'll go when you are finished," she said.

Matthew pushed the pan away from him. "Take this grub out of here. If we need anything, we'll ask Big Nellie at the saloon."

"Yes, sir," she said, deeply hurt.

Will looked sympathetic but he wouldn't contradict his boss. He carried her basket out to the wagon.

"I wish he wouldn't treat me like a helpless child."

Will looked embarrassed. "That's his way, Mrs. Jake."

"I wouldn't have taken any unnecessary risks," she said, "and the outlaw's poor mother should know what's happened to him."

"You'd better do as Matthew says," Will replied soberly.

"I will," she said, "but under protest." She picked up the handle on her wagon and started up the street.

Chapter Eight

THE CITIZENS OF Ragtown talked of little else but the trial of the Kid as they waited for the circuit judge to arrive. This would be the first murder trial in Ragtown since Nevada became a state in 1864. The hangman's scaffolding had already been built.

The excitement that ran through the town reminded Rosy of a country fair. She saw nothing to celebrate. Hopefully, the judge would arrive soon before some of the citizens took the law into their own hands.

She would be called to testify, of course. She'd identified the Kid and Jake's gun and would do so for the court. Sheriff Kincaid had a solid case against the Kid.

As Rosy and Aunt Hester walked to the Mercantile, they saw a stranger arrive in town on a big roan. He was a portly gentleman dressed in a black suit and wearing a string tie.

He saw them and tipped his hat.

Rosy nodded but Hester tightened her grip on Rosy's arm.

"Hello, ladies," the man said as he dismounted. He tied his horse to a hitching post. "My name is Lowell Benson. I'm a lawyer and I'm here to represent the defendant."

This was a surprise. Someone had hired a lawyer for the Kid.

"Pleased to meet you," Rosy replied. It was always

important to show good manners. She couldn't help but wonder what Matthew would say to the man.

"Could you ladies direct me to the nearest boardinghouse?" he asked.

Auntie remained tight-lipped. She didn't like the man, Rosy could tell.

"Why, yes I can, Mr. Benson," Rosy said. "The two story building at the end of the street is Ragtown's finest hotel."

Mr. Benson tipped his hat again. "If you ladies would excuse me, I need to go and wash off some of this dust."

He did know how to act in polite society but Rosy couldn't help but wonder if he was a snake in the grass.

Rosy said good day. Matthew stood in the doorway of the sheriff's office looking at them. Certainly there wasn't any harm in her talking to Mr. Benson? Her temperature still soared when she thought of his rude treatment when she'd expressed the slightest bit of compassion for the prisoner.

Their relationship had been less than cordial ever since.

Maybe Hester was right. Maybe she and Matthew were too unalike.

When they reached the Mercantile, Jason came bounding out the door carrying a package wrapped in brown paper.

"Gracious, me," Hester exclaimed.

"Sorry, ma'am," Jason said.

"Where are you off to?" Rosy asked, always delighted to see the boy.

"I'm delivering these new bibles to the minister," Jason replied, walking backward. He remembered to tip his flat cap to the ladies.

The opening of school had been postponed until the

trial was over so the court could use the new schoolhouse for the trial. Rosy was deservingly proud the school was being used for this purpose. Ragtown was a community with laws and principles. Outlaws would do well to change their behavior when passing through.

"There's a good boy," Aunt Hester said, mollified.

Jason grinned and turned. He ran up the street.

"Such exuberance," Hester said. "Such energy."

Auntie had been in a very good mood these past few days. Rosy had to believe Angus McFarland had something to do with the lady's exceptional cheerfulness, although Aunt Hester hadn't admitted as much. The stagecoach driver had become a regular fixture at their house, taking his tea in the parlor with Hester.

He'd left with the stage that morning and Hester had gotten up early to see him off.

There was a change in her, Rosy reflected, a change close to happiness.

A little bell jingled as she and Hester entered the Mercantile. Mr. Turner looked up and removed his reading glasses. Rosy had decided that Hester needed a new dress and the fabrics of a bygone era wouldn't do.

Hester had protested but Rosy prevailed. The two ladies were on a shopping trip.

One of Mr. Turner's bright calicos or gaily-colored ginghams would be perfect.

"Good morning, ladies," Mr. Turner said cheerfully.

"Good morning," Rosy answered.

Hester looked around with some trepidation. The Mercantile not only sold dress material and sewing notions but also an array of farm implements and firearms. There were barrels of pickles and fifty pound bags of cornmeal. Mr. Turner carried just about anything a person could ask for.

Hester looked as if she'd stepped into a foreign land. There were some things about Hester that would never change, Rosy decided.

"How can I help you?" Mr. Turner asked.

"I would like some needles and thread," Rosy said.

Mr. Turner indicated the display of dry goods with pride. "I don't mind telling you, you won't find any better selection anywhere in the state."

"Also I need a pound of sugar and a pound of coffee," she said as she looked over the display.

He nodded and went behind the counter to measure out her order.

Hester examined the bolts of fabric. She frowned at the selection until a bolt of medium blue cotton caught her attention. She ran her hand over the material.

"That looks to be your color," Rosy said with encouragement.

"I don't know," Hester said.

"It's very good quality," Mr. Turner said from behind the counter.

"Yes, indeed. I can tell," Rosy said. "What do you think, Auntie?"

Hester hesitated. Rosy saw her glance at the manila card that indicated the price per yard. They hadn't talked about finances but Rosy guessed that her auntie had very little money of her own.

"We'll take two and a half yards of the blue cotton," Rosy said firmly even though she'd no money to pay for it. "Put it on my account, if you please."

"I can't let you buy this for me," Hester said weakly. It was a show for Mr. Turner.

"I promised you a new dress ages ago. You'll need something new to wear to the trial."

"This cotton would make a nice dress," Hester said, admitting to her own desire.

She looked at Mr. Turner. "We do want to look our best."

Mr. Turner nodded. "Yes, indeed."

"Then it's settled." Rosy put the coffee and sugar in her basket.

Mr. Turner measured out the fabric, cut it off the bolt and folded it neatly. He wrapped the bundle in brown paper, tied it with string and handed the package to her aunt.

"I ordered those slates and pencils like you asked," Mr. Turner said as he opened the door for them.

"Thank you." Rosy hadn't forgotten. "I look forward to the school year starting."

Mr. Turner looked pleased. She knew how much he set store by his son and, she'd no doubt, Jason would be the first to arrive.

"It seems everything has come to a standstill waiting for the wheels of justice to turn," he said.

"I quite agree," Rosy replied. She was anxious for the whole business to be over.

Mr. Turner looked up at the sky. "Nice weather for a hanging."

Rosy grimaced. It was the way people talked in Ragtown, making light of death and dying. "Good day, Mr. Turner."

They walked down the boardwalk on their way home when they saw a carriage coming down the street drawn by a black horse. A white haired man drove the vehicle.

"Looks like the judge has arrived from Carson," Rosy said to Hester. They watched as the man continued down the street.

"There will be justice in this town and with justice, order," Hester said.

Rosy grasped Auntie by the elbow and gave her a squeeze. They continued down the boardwalk. Even though it gave Rosy no satisfaction that her husband's killer would hang, for hang he must, she must agree with Hester and the others. Justice would firm the town's foundation and would bring civilized people a measure of well-deserved peace.

THE CITIZENS OF Ragtown filed into the school in their Sunday best. The men who could afford to wore jackets. The others wore freshly washed flannel or cotton shirts and carried their hats in their hands.

The ladies had put on their best clothes and millinery. Rosy was grateful that her dress covered her growing stomach. She hadn't told anyone except Hester about the baby but she couldn't keep her secret much longer.

A table and chair had been set in front of the room with a row of chairs facing the table. Another chair had been set to the side for witnesses. This was the best they could do since Ragtown didn't have a proper courthouse like they did in Carson City. It would be enough.

As Hester chatted with Mrs. Turner, Rosy watched the door for Matthew and the prisoner. She wasn't the only one. The crowd grew more animated in anticipation of the sheriff and his charge. The ladies fanned themselves and the men struggled with too tight collars and the room began to close in on Rosy. She stood on wobbly feet.

"Are you all right?" Hester asked.

"I need some fresh air," Rosy replied.

"I'll go with you," Hester said.

"There's no need," Rosy said.

She excused herself and made her way to the door where young Jason stood peering out. He'd washed his flyaway hair and it was parted down the middle still wet. She thought how handsome he looked and how some day he'd break hearts but now at the tender age of twelve, he was her devoted student. She loved him like her own brother.

"Pa says there's going to be a hanging," Jason said eagerly.

"He's right," she replied, not sure if she could be happy. A life for a life, the Bible said. The Kid had wasted his.

She couldn't stop thinking about the Kid's request to send a letter to his mother. A letter home seemed like such a small consideration. Matthew had been inflexible in not granting his last wish. Rosy thought he'd been unfair if not to the prisoner then to his grieving family. Didn't his mother deserve to know what happened to her son? Shouldn't she be spared the years of agony wondering if he was dead or alive?

The Kid would be dead soon and it would be too late.

She saw Matthew leave the sheriff's office and disappear into the saloon. No doubt Will and Barney guarded the prisoner. She'd have no trouble handling the two deputies.

This was a chance to give the Kid his dying wish.

"Jason," she said. "There's something I need to do at the sheriff's office."

"Do you want me to take you over there?" the boy asked, protectively.

"No. I'll manage fine. You wait here. If my aunt asks, will you tell her where I've gone?"

"Yes, Ma'am."

She crossed the street quickly and entered the office.

What she saw stunned her.

Will Cannon was crouched at the prisoner's feet, unlocking the iron shackles around the Kid's ankles as the Kid strapped on a six-shooter. Barney, bound and gagged, squirmed on the cot in the cell.

"What are you doing?" she cried.

"You shouldn't have come," Will said, looking up.

"I don't understand," she replied.

Will stood and brushed off his hands. "Go away, Mrs. Jake. Go and don't tell a soul what you've seen here."

Rosy began to get a clear picture of what happened the morning Jake had been killed.

"You let this man out of the cell that morning," she said.

There was deep sorrow in Will's gaze. "You gotta believe me. I didn't know there'd be a shooting."

"Why would you do such a thing?"

Will's face was stricken with grief. "The Kid is my brother."

"Blood is thicker than water, ain't that right, Will?" the Kid said.

Rosy stepped back. Her hand touched the rough metal of the door handle.

Quick as lightening, the Kid grabbed her arm. "Not so fast. You're my guaranteed safe passage out of this nothing town."

His fingers dug into her arm. Rosy let out a yelp.

"Let her go," Will pleaded. He looked like he was going to be sick.

Rosy knew what the Kid was capable of. She knew he'd kill a man as easily as he'd swat a fly. She had to keep her wits about her so she could pull free of his grasp.

She flailed at him with her left arm but he caught her before she landed a blow to his head. He didn't flinch, in fact, he looked like he enjoyed her distress.

The door opened. Matthew stood in the doorway holding a tray with tin mugs of coffee and slabs of buttered bread. The tray made an awful clatter as it hit the floor. The mugs bounced and coffee spattered in every direction.

In the blink of any eye, the Kid drew his weapon. "Out of my way, Sheriff, or this pretty little gal will get hurt."

Rosy froze with fear. Her gaze connected with Matthew's. His eyes were very dark, like a gathering storm.

"Don't do anything stupid," he said to the Kid.

The Kid smirked. "Shuck your weapon."

Matthew took his gun out of the holster and dropped it on the floor.

"Kick it under the desk," the Kid said.

Matthew did as he was told.

"Now put your hands up," he said.

Matthew eyes narrowed.

"Do it," the Kid gripped Rosy tighter. "Or she gets a bullet through her head."

Matthew raised his hands. His gaze never wavered from the Kid.

"You go outside nice and easy," the Kid told Matthew.

Matthew went out with his hands above his head.

The Kid pushed her toward the door. When they reached the opening, Rosy saw they were surrounded by men with their weapons drawn, including Jason.

"Jason," Rosy said. The situation was more than a boy his age could handle. "Go back to the school. I'll be all right. This man will take me to the edge of town and release me. No one will be hurt."

ROSY

The Kid wrapped his arm around her neck and pressed the cold steel of Will's Colt to her temple.

Rosy tried to breathe but she couldn't draw in a lung full of air. Her hands flew to her throat but she couldn't dislodge his grip.

They faced the men.

"Step aside or I'll kill her," he said, his hot breath hitting her cheek. His tone had turned serious. Deadly serious.

Matthew stayed calm. His expression registered neither shock nor surprise. "Let's not get all riled," he said evenly.

She needed that from him. Close to panic, she feared she would faint. She concentrated on his face, drawing strength from his strength.

"This is what we're going to do if you want this little lady to live," the Kid said.

Will Cannon wrung his hands as his gaze darted from Matthew to his brother. He hadn't drawn a weapon.

"Put those Winchesters on the ground," the Kid said.

The Kid left them no choice. Jason and the men put their guns on the ground. Rosy sputtered as his arm crushed her windpipe and she struggled for air.

"Don't hurt her," Jason cried out. Before anyone could stop him, the boy jumped on the Kid's back, pounding with both fists.

Jason was quick but the Kid was stronger and an experienced fighter. He landed an elbow in the boy's face. Jason fell in the dirt. His nose began to bleed.

Rosy tried to scream but the sound strangled in her throat. She hated him for what he was doing. She hated herself for giving him the chance.

"If you know what's good for you, you'll stay put," he told the boy.

95

Jason glared as he wiped blood from his face with the back of his hand but he stayed put.

Rosy blinked rapidly. She was afraid for herself and her unborn child and she was terrified for Jason. Life had become such a fragile thread. She couldn't let any harm come to those she loved.

Folks spilled out of the schoolhouse. When they saw Matthew with his hands in the air and Rosy struggling, they realized what was happening. The men helped the women and children back into the building.

"You hightail it out of here," Matthew said, after everyone was safely inside. "Nobody'll interfere. There's no reason to take the lady."

"I've got no score to settle with you, Sheriff. As far as I'm concerned, you're as good as it gets fighting with the Union Army like you done. You'll agree that Jake Sherry had it coming to him, being a Johnny Reb and all."

Matthew didn't react but maintained his composure, like a panther waiting to strike. "The war is over."

"Maybe so but this little girl is bounty." A chuckle rose out of the Kid's chest. The sound wasn't lighthearted but cruel.

"There's no reason for anybody to get hurt," Matthew said. "Let her go and you can ride."

"Being Sherry's woman, she's a choice piece." The Kid snorted. "I aim to have a little fun with her."

Jason was fit to be tied. He lunged for the Winchester.

Rosy stomped on the Kid's foot and spun out of his grasp. Fire spat out of the barrel of the Colt and a bullet roared past her.

Jason lay on the ground, his blood pooling in the dirt. Rosy screamed, a sound feral and wild. The Kid tried to grab her but she ducked. He caught her sleeve and the fabric ripped.

She hurried to Jason's side. She saw with horror the bullet had gone through his left eye and exited behind his right ear.

The Kid held the gun on her as she knelt next to Jason. The Kid meant to take her with him. He would kill anyone who got in the way.

Her hand was inches from the stock of Jason's rifle. She looked up at the Kid. He breathed hard, a murderous rage possessing him. He'd kill her before she'd a chance to pick it up and fire.

"You're through," Matthew said.

The Kid swung his gun around on Matthew. His expression was pitiless. "Who says?"

"I say."

"I'm gonna enjoy killing you, Sheriff." He thumbed back the hammer.

Rosy grabbed the Winchester and gripped the trigger. The gun went off and kicked back into her chest. The Kid's hands went up and he fell backward. Matthew lunged at him and the two men fought. As Matthew tried to wrestle the gun from his hand, Rosy stood. Blood streamed from the Kid's leg as he and Matthew rolled on the ground.

She stepped on the Kid's flailing hand, putting a stop to the fight.

Matthew sprang to his feet, holding the Colt. Rosy pointed the Winchester at the Kid but she knew the shooting was over.

"Are you all right?" Matthew asked.

She blew a tendril of hair off her face. "I've been better."

Relief spread across his face. "Next time aim higher."

He hauled the Kid to a sitting position.

She dropped the rifle on the ground. Dr. McKinnon came running. He took one look at Jason and shook his head. He shrugged out of his jacket and handed it over to Rosy.

"I don't want this boy's mother to see him like this," he said.

She covered the boy's face. She'd never been so afraid but fear was nothing compared to her sorrow.

Matthew kept a tight hold on the Kid while the doctor examined his leg.

"The leg's broken," he told Matthew.

"Patch him up. He's got a date with the hangman." He turned to Will. "Make that two."

Rosy couldn't face him. She'd defied his order to stay way from the Kid and now Jason was dead. She was ready to collapse.

Matthew Kincaid made no effort to comfort her.

He directed the Ragtown citizens to remove Jason's body and he slapped a pair of handcuffs on Will.

Doc wrapped the Kid's leg up with a cotton bandage.

Matthew would never forgive her. With more sadness than anyone should have to carry, Rosy walked away.

Chapter Nine

A FTER DR. MCKINNON patched the Kid up, the trial continued. Rosy testified, her voice trembling. The judge thanked her and she left the courtroom. Outside, she took a deep cleaning breath. The streets were empty. Jason's blood stained the ground.

Rosy headed for the Mercantile to help Alice Turner lay out her boy for a funeral.

She'd no doubt that justice would be done. There were plenty of witnesses to Jason Turner's murder. Matthew would do his duty and carry out the sentence.

That was little comfort with the boy dead.

Rosy washed Jason's body with rose-scented water. She cleansed the hideous wound, the hole where his left eye had been.

Jason had grown since she'd arrived in Ragtown. She saw the man he might have been.

Alice combed his wet hair.

"He was a good boy," Rosy said.

"He wanted to be a sheriff when he grew up," Alice replied. She planted a kiss on his forehead. They dressed him in clean clothes—a cotton shirt, wool vest and wool pants.

Rosy heard Mr. Turner out back pounding nails into lumber for a coffin.

Matthew came into the store to tell them the verdict.

Rosy had already guessed when she heard hollering and whooping on both sides of the main street.

Rosy sighed. "What will happen to Will?"

"He'll hang, along with his brother."

Alice sniffed.

Matthew covered his chest with his hat and looked at the boy. He took off his badge and pinned it on Jason's vest.

Alice hurried to the back storeroom, her handkerchief clutched to her mouth.

Rosy thought she would collapse. She didn't. Alice needed her. She wouldn't let her down.

"I'd better get back," Matthew said.

"Thank you for letting us know about the verdict."

"Rosy," he said.

"I can't talk about his right now but I am sorry. I'm so very sorry."

"Don't blame yourself."

Rosy squeezed her eyes shut. The stabbing pain of guilt would always be there. "I should've listened to you."

He took hold of her by the arms. She shook her head and turned away. He let her go. She heard the door shut and his footsteps on the boardwalk.

THE PEOPLE OF Ragtown laid Jason Turner to rest in a pine coffin at the emigrant cemetery on a grassy knoll above the town. The preacher said some kind words. They all sang tunes remembered from childhood. Every citizen tried to comfort the Turners the best they could.

Rosy thought of her precious baby and the perils of bringing up a child in this wilderness. As she walked arm and arm with Hester down the slope toward town, her grief made each step painful.

Matthew stood at the edge of the gathering, his hat in his hand. Everyone in town agreed he was tough and brave. Even Hester had commented favorably on his abilities as a lawman.

Today he looked vulnerable. Jason's death had hit him hard.

Rosy patted Hester's hand. "I need to go talk to the sheriff."

Hester nodded. Ever since she'd told Hester how she felt about Matthew, Hester hadn't said another word against the man.

Rosy knew Matthew would be leaving soon and she had to let him know she would never forget him. She left Hester and went to him. They stood under the shade of a cottonwood watching the others walk back to town.

"I wish there could be an end to the killing," she said.

He took her hand in his. It was unexpected and she was grateful he didn't hold a grudge.

"Maybe one day but not today," he said. "The memories of the War are still too fresh in our minds."

She looked up into his warm eyes. "I want to be forgiving."

He pulled her into his arms. She didn't resist and rested her head on his broad chest. "Forgiveness is a start."

"Can you forgive me for what I've done?"

"You did what a lady would do." He kissed the top of her bonnet.

She tilted her head up. She saw only love in his gaze.

"I've traveled many a hard road but maybe it's time for me to settle down," he said.

"I'm glad to hear you say so."

"I'm mighty partial to your cooking and all. These past few weeks, even a man like me gets used to a woman's gentling ways."

"What are you getting at, Matthew Kincaid?"

"The long and the short of it is it'd please me mightily if you'd consent to be my wife."

She touched his face. She loved him. She'd do anything and everything in her power to quiet the demons that raged inside him.

"You haven't answered me, Rosy girl."

She stood on her toes and kissed him. "I would like nothing better."

A grin spread across his face. She placed her hand over his mouth. "Before you say anything, there's something you should know."

He kissed each fingertip. It was a distraction that weakened her resolve. She didn't want to lose this moment. After all, he'd find out soon enough.

"What is it you have to say?" he asked, placing her hand on his chest.

"I'm going to have a baby."

He stepped back and gave her a thorough looking over. "Could'a fooled me. Of course, I'm no expert."

"Will it matter that I'm carrying Jake's baby? Because if it does, you need to tell me now."

He rested his boot on a rock and studied the horizon where the mountains met the sky. "There's something you should know about me."

She rested her hand on his shoulder.

"I grew up in an orphanage in New York," he said. "I wouldn't wish that upbringing on any child."

"You lost your family when you were young," she said. It explained a lot about him.

"Pa ran off and never came back. Ma died of a broken heart."

"You were alone?"

"I have an older brother but I don't know where he is. He's a lot like my old man." He straightened.

"Is that his watch you keep in your vest?" she asked.

He patted his vest pocket as if to reassure himself that the watch was still there.

"Yes, ma'am."

Rosy hugged him as if she'd never let him go. "Thank you for telling me."

He stroked her hair. "That baby should have a proper home and a ma and pa. I mean to be its pa."

"Are you sure?" she asked, letting him go. She'd no doubt he'd make a good father but she had to ask the question. She had to be certain.

"Darlin', I've never been more sure of anything in my life."

She believed him. "Then the answer is yes."

He kissed her on the mouth and she returned his kiss. She'd never thought she'd find love again but it was here for the taking.

Living out here in the wilderness was full of hardship and loss. The lessons came hard. She'd made mistakes. She'd make more.

An endearing love gave her what she needed.

Rosy was ready to begin again.

Dear Readers,

Come take a journey with me to Edwardian England and the American West where feisty heroines and the men they love find adventure and their happily ever after.

I write romance and strive to infuse each character with the personal courage and commitment to take the journey of self-discovery that will make them worthy to love. How my characters arrive at their destinations continues to amaze me.

My background is as American as apple pie. I was born and raised in northern Michigan, graduated from the University of Michigan, and worked as a Peace Corps Volunteer in Kenya.

Today my husband and I live in San Diego, the place of my heart, close to our beautiful children and grandchild.

I welcome your comments and I hope you'll join me on social media. Let me know what you are reading and what kinds of books you like.

With thanks,
Sarah

Facebook: facebook.com/sarahrichmondwriter
Twitter: twitter.com/srichmondwriter
Goodreads:
goodreads.com/author/show/1725233.Sarah_Richmond

Books about the American West by Sarah Richmond

Dulcie Crowder Gets Her Man

Brides of Serendipity
Courtin' Dory
Barrett's Law
Rosy
Angels with Dirty Faces

Also by Sarah Richmond

Rose Adagio
Past Forgetting
A Most Ineligible Suitor
Do Be Sensible, Miss Wynchcomb
A Perilous Proposal: Book One in the House of Caruthers series
A Secret Engagement: Book Two in the House of Caruthers series
A Wayward Wedding: Book Three in the House of Caruthers series
Running on Empty
Mrs. Pratt's War

Find out more at **www.SarahRichmond.com**

www.ingramcontent.com/pod-product-compliance
Lightning Source LLC
Chambersburg PA
CBHW030554130626
46552CB00006B/2549